The Dreaming

Gina Briganti

This book is a work of fiction. Any resemblance to actual persons, places, or events, real or imagined, are intended for your enjoyment only and should not be taken as fact.

First Printing
ISBN:1450578276
EAN 13: 9781450578271
Copyright © 2012
Cover design by www.humblenations.com

No part of this work may be reproduced or used in any form, by any means, graphic, electronic, or mechanical, including photocopying, recording, taping, and information retrieval systems, without the prior written permission of Gina Briganti.

Also by Gina Briganti

<u>Non-Fiction</u>
Keep It Simple:
Permission to Illuminate Your Life
Easily, Effortlessly & Joyfully

DEDICATION

I dedicate this book to my children Antonina and Vincent. Thank you for being patient while my head was in The Dreaming, and for giving feedback when I asked for it. You have each given this book a special flavor. I love you!

Thank you to Lynn Burton for being the best friend a writer can ask for. You encourage and inspire me in countless ways.

Thank you, Ann, for reading over the parts about horses. Your relationship with horses is inspiring.

Chapter 1

"I will choose that one." A silver haired man spoke to a woman holding a clipboard.

"Choose me? What do you mean choose me?" Dana looked around at her unfamiliar surroundings. Where was she? Shouldn't she be in her bed, at home, asleep?

The question did not produce a response from either of them. She watched the man exchange a piece of paper with the woman before he turned to look at Dana again.

"Let's go." He turned to walk out. Following him seemed like the best choice so she did.

"Where are we going?" She noted that they were gliding, not walking, on hover boards. "Scratch the 'where are we going,' and tell me where we are. Please." Her automatic training kicked in, demanding manners.

"Don't you know?" He spoke to the air in front of him, eyes straight ahead. Sarcasm bubbled up her throat, wanted to pop through her lips, but she held it back. "No." Dana hoped she sounded polite.

"You are in The Dreaming." The silver haired man continued forward on his hover board. His board turned left. Hers did, too.

"What is The Dreaming?" Her curiosity was waking up. Was this a lucid dream? She knew what to do with those. She had lots of practice.

"You've used 4 questions, you have only 16 remaining."

Hmm. Not knowing how long she was going to be wherever she was she started to observe instead of asking another question he might not answer.

They stopped in front of a tiny building. So tiny she thought of leprechauns.

The man touched the key pad in front of what appeared to be a door. The door slid upward. The boards carried them forward.

"You will be working here, in the kitchen."

The man started to leave the room.

"Please, wait." Dana searched her mind for a way to gain as much information as she could out of a single question.

"Yes?" He turned to look at her. As she watched his green eyes looking into hers it crossed her mind that it would be cool if his eyes were a deeper green. His eyes shifted to a deeper green. Whoa. Her own eyes widened as the green became the exact shade she was imagining.

The Dreaming

"Please tell me exactly what you would like for me to do because I don't have any clue about The Dreaming. This kitchen looks clean to me."

The room they stood in was round. There were clear tubes coming out of the walls every 5 feet, each ending in a metal tray. The entire wall was covered in luxurious purple silk. There were no other furnishings.

"A dinner bot will be here shortly to carry meals to the patrons. You will order the food here and give it to her." The man did not smile. His tone was matter-of-fact. He was dressed in a flowing white robe, his arms covered to his wrists, the bottom of it sweeping the floor. She guessed him to be about 8 feet tall.

The thought crossed her mind that he was too tall, and as it did he began to shrink. When he had diminished to around six feet she thought, o*h no, no, stop!*

He immediately stopped shrinking. His expression didn't reflect that anything had changed.

Puzzled, but confident that everything could still work out well, a flash of insight came to her. "Can I please have more questions?"

The silver haired man blinked at her, silently.

What she assumed was a dinner bot came through an opening bearing a tray and a three foot long list trailing off of it. She stood six feet tall and looked like any waitress she would normally imagine. "Orders," she said in a robotic monotone.

She reached for the list, noting that it was not in English. She thought it looked like French and wished then that she had paid more attention when various opportunities to learn the language had presented themselves. She looked at the list again, thinking that her extreme interest in food might help her to understand the list.

Nope.

She wished the list was in English. She looked down at the list again. It was now in English.

Tension started to roll off her, her confidence building. She could do this! Gosh darn it!

The three of them stood there for what felt like hours. Nothing happened. She considered whether or not to ask another question. There was, after all, no guarantee that she would get an answer.

She studied the clear tubes in the walls that ended in metal trays, and the list she now held in her hand. It seemed that the food must come down the tubes. Her logical mind laughed at her. Why would any of this qualify as logical?

She might as well give it a try. The first order was chicken and dumplings, Perrier, and a slice of apple pie a la mode. She stood in front of one of the tubes and visualized the order coming down and settling on the tray.

The Dreaming

The Perrier appeared on one tray with a clear glass of ice beside it.

The apple pie a la mode appeared on another tray.

The chicken and dumplings on another.

The dinner bot collected the items and left through the doorway, gliding down a long hallway she couldn't see the end of once the dinner bot took the right hand turn.

She looked at the next order and "thought" it down the tubes. There it was! She was filled with confidence again. She knew she could do this.

The list was long, and the dinner bot wasn't back. Hmm. She decided to "think" another order onto the trays, and another, until the trays were full.

She looked at the motionless silver haired man. "Dinner bot," she said, in a tone that couldn't be thought of as a question.

The dinner bot appeared in the room, sprouting arms for all the orders and disappearing down the long hallway again. She returned bearing all empty dishes and a new list.

Dana knew they were only halfway through the first list. "Man," she thought, "if I wanted to work this hard I would just wake up."

"Wake up!" One of her sweet 16 year olds was shaking her. "I can't find my blue plaid jacket and I told Jim I would wear it today."

The dregs of the dream dissolved into the

familiar surroundings of her own king sized, pillow topped mattress with the iron head and foot board she adored. She was wearing her cozy faux suede green sweats. And she was, thankfully, no longer doing kitchen duty in The Dreaming.

She thought about how odd her dream was as she told Jenny where she had hung her "missing" sweatshirt in her closet. She kept her tone neutral, knowing the day would be smoother if they didn't start it the way she was tempted to start it.

Her mind flashed over the day ahead while she stood in the shower, deliciously warm water sluicing down her body as she lathered with her favorite vanilla scented body wash.

She could hear her son, Jason, in the other shower, getting ready for the day. They would be zooming down the street to school soon. Not together. They were vetoing ride sharing lately. Her suggestion that they should keep sharing expenses was met with the answer that since they had jobs and paid for the gas they should be able to choose if they went together or not.

Dana stood in front of her kitchen window, watching Peaches and Cream play in the backyard.

The golden retrievers were litter mates that she and the twins had been given as puppies by her parents.

The Dreaming

The day before her was full of cooking and writing. She had a deadline and she was glad that if she missed it she wouldn't actually end up dead. She might wish she was, though.

The sleek notebook computer in front of her held her notes for the latest incarnation of "Dana Cooks." The new cookbook was "Dana Cooks for Company" and promised to make impressing your guests easy. She was almost out of the testing phase now. The copy was written. Other unlucky people on the team were figuring out the nuts and bolts of photographing the food. She pinched herself thinking that she was now in the final stages of her 7th book and her fans were anxious to own it.

Thank goodness she had Jason and his friends to help eat the food when she was testing because if they wouldn't eat it nobody would. Their enormous appetites appealed to her sense of economy, too, because there was rarely anything to throw away.

The hours melted by as she chopped, washed, cooked, noted, and tasted her creations, refining them to the perfection she was famous for.

Brittany arrived as she put the last test batch in the freezer for the notes on which dishes would freeze well. Brittany was her on-call maid for days like this. The kitchen was destroyed. Brittany was happy to clean it for $10.00 an hour and food to take with her.

They sat together at the table tasting the chocolate mint cheesecake she had finally nailed. Brittany was making sounds of pleasure and licking her fork for nonexistent crumbs, saving her a precious question.

Where did that come from?

Brittany collected her food and payment, taking a last look over everything before she took off. "Should I come by early next Wednesday to clean the house?"

Dana nodded. "That's perfect for me. Just plan to do the kitchen last. I'll be around the whole day, so just come over when it's convenient for you. Thanks, Brittany. It's so much easier with your help."

"Thank you, Dana. And thanks for telling your friend about me. She hired me so now I have three houses. That's all I need to round out my expenses."

"I'm glad. I still remember eating too much ramen and peanut butter in college. It doesn't always have to be that tight."

Brittany waved a last cheery goodbye and let herself out.

Jason and his friends arrived with their reliable appetites. Dana watched them move down the table, loading their plates, passing up the questionable looking butternut squash chili she knew tasted great.

A new face smiled at her uncertainly as he looked at all the options on the table.

"I'm Dana," she smiled to welcome him. "Jason's

mom. Please help yourself to anything you like. You're doing me a favor by eating it."

"Yeah, Carter, eat up man. We do this every week." Jeremy, Jason's best friend since third grade told him while tasting a roasted vegetable infused rice. "Good one, Mrs. C."

Half an hour later the table was considerably lighter and she had a lot of notes on the latest versions of her recipes. She relaxed for the first time in hours.

She heard the doorbell ring and listened to see if Jason was going to get it.

She was getting it.

"Just a minute." She peered through the peep hole at the unfamiliar man on her front porch holding a cowboy hat in his hand. He must be the new guy's dad.

"Hello," she smiled, thinking unflattering things about what she must look like after a full day in the kitchen. He, on the other hand, looked tired and smelled wonderful.

"I'm Joe. I'm here to pick up Carter." Joe shifted his weight, hoping to look casual while he tried not to notice how gorgeous she was.

"It's lovely to meet you, Joe. I'm Dana Carapelli. The kids call me Mrs. C." She pushed hair off her face and held out a hand to shake. "I'll get Carter for you. Have you eaten? We have food if you're hungry."

She was excited at the idea of an adult test subject. Maybe the lonely orange chili would have a fan before the night was over.

"I'm starving. Normally I wouldn't want to impose but we're still getting settled in at our place and I don't want another burger." He followed her into the kitchen. "It smells incredible in here."

His eyes went wide when he saw the orange chili.

He carefully stepped away from it. She laughed as she handed him a plate. "Take what you like. What can I get you to drink? I have water, coffee, tea, juice, and beer."

Joe was proving his bravery and chivalry by taking a small spoonful of the orange chili.

"I'd love a beer." He sat at the kitchen table, looking around uncertainly, just as his son had.

"We've all eaten. My daughter Jenny is at work and there's plenty left for her. Kick back, relax. I'll go find Carter."

Dana followed the noise to Jason's bedroom.

They were playing virtual baseball and one of her least favorite screamo bands. Loud.

"Carter, your dad is here. He just sat down to eat so you have a few minutes before you need to go." She waved her hands around and yelled at the top of her lungs, pointing at Carter for emphasis.

The Dreaming

"K, Mrs. C., I'll be right there."

She escaped back to the relative quiet of the kitchen. Joe had eaten the orange chili.

"He's on his way out. So, what do you think?" She leaned against the counter.

Joe flushed a little at what he was thinking. Dana was a nice, neighborly sort of woman. She didn't need him thinking about what she looked like naked.

She preened with the awareness that he found her attractive. She winked at him. "Of the food."

Joe's tanned face widened into a big smile, his blue eyes taking on a new shine.

"I think my son made an excellent choice of friends in Jason Carapelli." He swigged the last of his beer, watching appreciatively while Dana reached for a glass from the cupboard. She filled it with water and handed it to him.

"I hear you two moved in a couple of weeks ago. Are you finding everything alright?" She glanced at the clock, then back at Joe. "Hold that thought, hurricane Jenny is due any minute."

On cue Jenny burst through the door connecting the garage and the kitchen, giving Joe a glimpse of a clean, organized garage.

"Mom, I got you the cutest sandals. Look!" Jenny held out a pair of black flip flops with silver flowers on the straps. "They were $4.00 with my discount."

She took the sandals, her mouth breaking into a wide smile. "Thanks, Jenny. These will look great with my new sun dress." She stepped in to hug Jenny.

"Jenny, we have a few people over. This is Joe, Carter's dad. Joe, this is Jenny."

Jenny turned to say hello to Joe, instantly picking up on the fact that he was cozy here in the kitchen with her mom. Way to go, mom!

"Hi, Joe." She eyed the plate in front of him. "Another test subject. Cool." With that Jenny went to her room to deposit her books and bags.

He looked back to Dana where she stood holding the sandals. "I'm a test subject?"

"Poison control insists." Why not show him her dorky sense of humor?

Joe chuckled, rising with his plate as Carter entered the room.

Seeing them standing together was proof positive that they were father and son. Carter was just a younger version of Joe.

"I've got all my stuff, dad. I finished some of my math homework, too. Thanks again for all the food, Mrs. C. It's really good."

Dana appreciated his attempt to show off his manners for his dad. "You are very welcome. Wednesday is test day. You're invited, both of you, for next week."

"We'll be here. Thank you, Dana. It's been awhile since I had food this great. I like home cooking."

He put his dishes on the counter and looked around for the trash for his beer bottle. Dana held out a hand. "I recycle those." She motioned to the door. "I'll walk you out."

"No need, Dana. We'll see you next week."

They wore matching grins as they walked out the front door.

Chapter 2

Jenny looked over the offerings on the kitchen counter. She was only slightly hungry but the vegetarian mushroom stroganoff her mom was working on was delicious enough to tempt her.

She took some of it out on the patio with her math homework, and the dogs, Peaches and Cream.

Jason disappeared into his room to do homework after Jeremy left.

Dana sealed and stored the leftovers and took a last swipe around the kitchen. And now, she thought, I'm free!

She settled into her favorite reading spot in the living room with the latest J.D. Robb. She loved Eve Dallas, Roarke, Mavis, Peabody, McNab. Heck, she loved everything about the series.

Peaches pushed a wet tennis ball into her hand.

"Where did you get this?" She looked over the backyard, confused that it was daylight when she knew the sun had set. There were lots of tennis balls on the ground beneath the tennis ball tree. That must be where Peaches got it from.

A tennis ball tree?

Her confused mind bucked at what her eyes were seeing. There were other differences, too, including a large dog house that wasn't usually there.

"Oh, I'm dreaming." A lot of her house was missing. The dog door that Peaches and Cream used to get to their parts of the house was where it should be.

Her kitchen was gone! Where would she work without her kitchen?

"What's wrong?" Peaches asked her.

"The kitchen is...you're talking to me?" She stared, astonished.

"I do it all the time. You mean all this time you haven't been listening to me? It's been four years Dana." Peaches sat on a lounge chair by the pool, facing her.

The admonishing tone reminded Dana of her dead husband Ben.

"Well," she took a defensive stance, "dogs don't talk. Normally." That was true, wasn't it?

"Cream, come here."

She watched Peaches closely, clearly hearing her say the words to Cream without moving her lips.

Cream ran and jumped up to sit on the lounge chair next to Peaches. "Yeah?"

"Dana doesn't listen when we talk to her. She doesn't know that her stroke of genius now known as sizzling rice three flavor soup came from us."

Dana heard the frustration and humor in Peach's tone. "I have to sit down." A chair appeared behind her. A lovely chair from a patio set she had recently seen at the sporting goods store when they bought Jason's new shoes for track. She felt she had a few minutes coming to her to adjust to what she was seeing.

A question bubbled up in her brain. "Who's responsible for the tennis ball tree?"

Peaches and Cream laughed, the sound of each of their laughs matching their personalities. Cream answered. "I saw a picture of one on Jason's computer so I brought it here. They're flavored. Want to try one? This one tastes like roast turkey."

Cream pushed the ball into her hand. She lifted it to her nose to sniff and found that it smelled like a really delicious roasted turkey.

"How did you get this to me so fast?" She asked Cream. "You were just on the chair." She made herself relax. There was nothing threatening here, it was just a really interesting dream. Flavored tennis balls growing on a tree in the side yard and talking with her dogs could be...enjoyable, fun.

Peaches answered. "Your belief that we have to walk from here to the tree and back doesn't exist here, same with the idea that we can't talk or that tennis balls don't grow on trees." Dana just shook her head.

Cream spoke up. "I didn't have to move across the yard like in 'real life' because I don't have to pretend here. See?" Cream vanished from where she had been sitting next to her feet and reappeared on the roof of the dog house.

"Jenny said you two want a dog house." She went to Cream to pet her, feeling really pleasant sensations swamp her as she stroked her soft fur. "She's right, isn't she?"

Cream made a sound that Dana would call a groan of pleasure, too busy enjoying the stroking to answer.

"Yes, and that's the one we want," Peaches answered for them.

"What did you mean when you said that you are responsible for my sizzling rice three flavor soup?"

She wondered if she had ever felt this calm just sitting and stroking Cream's neck.

"We were sitting with you in the den. You had a laptop open on your legs and you were brainstorming for 'Dana Cooks Chinese Food.' I remembered you talking about how much you loved the sizzling rice soup you had at the fancy place you went on your date so I reminded you."

Cream licked her hand affectionately as she

"spoke."

"How are you doing that? How can you talk and lick my hand at the same time?" She was feeling pretty amazed at the moment. She clearly remembered that day years ago when she wrote the basics of the soup that was now one of the most clearly successful recipes in the Dana Cooks series.

"You have fifteen questions remaining." The six foot tall, green-eyed, silver haired man from her last dream stood on his hover board above the covered pool.

Cream licked Dana's hand. Then her face. Peaches jumped up on the couch, waking her from the dream.

Chapter 3

Rows of dog treats faced Dana, staring her down. She had less than an hour before she needed to be at the high school for open house and they didn't have her dog's favorite treats.

She looked over the rows again. Roasted turkey, did they have anything with roasted turkey? Done! Now she could check out and get all the groceries home and unloaded in time for open house.

"Welcome, parents, to open house. We hope you'll enjoy visiting your children's classrooms and seeing the hard work and progress they've made this year. You'll have twenty minutes in each class before a passing bell sounds. Thank you for being a successful part of our team."

Dana was sitting in Jason's sixth period class when Joe rushed in looking flustered.

"Hi, Joe. You made it. Coach Landry hasn't started yet."

Joe was glad to see a familiar face, a beautiful familiar face.

"Hi." He sat on the bench next to Dana.

They hadn't seen each other since their meeting last week. Carter had been over to her place a couple of times but Jason had brought him home.

"I'm passing consent forms around for a fund raiser car wash we have coming up. The details are on the form. The forms are due back by the end of the week." Coach Landry launched into his twenty minutes.

Dana and Joe sat with the other six parents listening to the coach talk about what he had been doing with the track team over the past months.

Coach was a busy, energetic, ex-college football player who had decided that teaching was a better fit for him than a career in professional sports. He was well liked and considered to be a great asset to the school.

The final bell rang dismissing them as it dismissed their children every school day. Dana wondered how different it sounded for the coach if he closed his eyes when the bell rang. How obvious would it be for him that they were the parents and not the group of teenagers he saw every school day?

Dana watched Joe stand and approach Coach Landry. She was close enough to hear their conversation. Joe introduced himself as Carter's dad

The Dreaming

and asked about how Carter was fitting in with his new school.

"Dana, oh, Dana! I have a wonderful little story idea I'd like your opinion on." The chatty Vanessa was quite possibly going to maim herself in trying to get to Dana before she could escape.

Dana found her precious store of patience inside and called on some of it. She had known Vanessa for ages and she knew the best thing to do was to hear her out here and now. Otherwise Vanessa could make it a personal goal to have this conversation with her.

Dana fixed a pleasant smile on her face, remembering how helpful Vanessa had been over the years in her own way. "How are you, Vanessa? How's Jenny?"

Vanessa's flaming red nails and matching lips rose in a happy greeting. "I'm good. My crazy daughter has gone and pierced her nose. What are you gonna do with these kids?" She shook her head the way parents do when their children defy their own understanding.

The remnants of her childhood in the south came through the question she didn't expect an answer for.

"As I was sayin' I would love to tell you about my story idea. It's of the erotic persuasion." Her voice dipped into a conspiratorial tone on the word erotic.

What would Dana's no nonsense editor say about an erotic query? She kept a straight face as Joe joined them.

"Vanessa, my editor only works on cookbooks. By all means, I encourage you to pursue your idea but I don't have any words of wisdom for you."

"Couldn't you just read it once I write it? Give me your opinion, as a writer and all?"

Dana took the life raft she had been given. The odds that Vanessa would follow through and actually give her a story to read were pretty slim. "Sure, Vanessa, you know where to find me." Dana gave a little wave, stepping backwards to be very clear that she was ending their chat.

"Hey." Joe put a gentle hand against the small of her back to keep her from stepping on him.

She turned quickly. "Oops, I almost got you there."

"I'm fast on my feet. It comes from working with horses. If they get me I could be down for a long time."

Vanessa couldn't help herself. She would meet this man that Dana so obviously knew. Why, hadn't he walked right over to Dana and sat down next to her snug as a bug in a rug?

"Is everyone alright over here?" Vanessa the good Samaritan wanted to know.

Joe knew her in an instant. She was likely to

spread every word that was said between the three of them all over town. "Everything is fine," Joe rolled out his reassuring smile. "I don't believe we've met. I'm Joe Jacobs. My son and I just moved to Joshua Tree."

"I'm Vanessa Little. It's a pleasure to meet you." She laid a hand on his right wrist, feeling the tanned skin and dark hair. "I see you know Dana?"

Joe decided that word would be all over town before the night was over. He looked to Dana for help. Since this was her town he trusted that she would know how to handle the tender subject of how well they knew each other.

Dana felt mischief rise to her eyes. They were hidden from Vanessa, but clearly visible to Joe.

Joe's attraction for Dana graduated from interest to intent. He enjoyed a woman he could play with.

"Jason and Joe's son Carter are friends. That's how we met." Her eyes sparkled a different message to Joe. They said, "I'll play nice this time, we'll see about next time."

"Hmm-" Vanessa started to say when her cell phone rang. "Well it's nice meeting you, Joe. Bye, Dana." She rushed off to take her phone call.

They were the last ones in the gym.

"Will we be an item by morning?" Joe asked as they walked out.

Feeling playful, she answered in her impression

of a southern drawl. "She was the one touching you." She continued in a gossipy tone, "In front of everyone, including me, even though I was clearly sitting right next to you."

He laughed. "I need to head that one off at the pass. If we're seen having coffee Vanessa won't be able to say I made a move on her, right?"

"True...but then we'll be fanning the flames of any fires she starts."

"Do you want to be a coffee shop kindling or a restaurant kindling?"

He was clever. Dana considered him. Was he going to speak plainly if they sat together for coffee? It was early by her knowledge of men for him to declare an interest, much less declare an interest to the whole town that they were friendly enough to spend time together without the kids. In public. She gave him an out.

"Joe, this is a very small town. Maybe we should just say goodnight. You'll be over tomorrow night for the tasting, right?"

"Listen, Dana, I'm fine with everyone in town knowing that we had a cup of coffee and with eating at your house tomorrow. I know small towns. I grew up in one."

They were standing close together and talking about more than the weather by anyone's observation, so what the heck?

The Dreaming

"I know a little spot. It's next to Vons. Do you want to follow me over there?" Dana coached herself to be calm.

Joe nodded his agreement to follow her and they walked together to the parking lot, Dana stopping often to greet friends. She introduced Joe to everyone they came across.

Joe saw genuine respect in people's eyes as they spoke with Dana. His impression of her as an easy-going person was right.

Dana pointed out her blue minivan for Joe to follow.

"I'm in the Frontier." He pointed it out to her. There's only one Vons in town, right? A few blocks east of here on the north side of the highway?"

"That's the one and only Vons. Patisserie Chocolat is right next to Vons."

I can do this, I can do this, Dana coached herself silently. I can act normal in front of sexy Joe.

Minutes later they stepped from the blacktop onto the curb in front of the open door to the patisserie. He placed a gentlemanly hand under her elbow to assist her up the steps to the counter.

He stood back to consider the menu board. Fancy food. No surprise there. "What's good?"

Dana scrutinized the glossy fruit tarts, coffee cake squares, cream puffs, cookies, cake slices, and pie wedges. She leaned into him and quietly recommended, "Anything but the coffee cake. It's drier than breadcrumbs."

The shop was intimate, holding ten small tables. The walls were painted a welcoming beige and the borders were trimmed in a delicious shade of chocolate.

"I'm going for the tiramisu and the espresso." She reached into her purse to get out her wallet.

"Uh uh, my turn." Joe stilled her hand from opening her wallet. "You fed us last time."

Proof that the seemingly nice guy actually WAS a nice guy spread a happy smile across her face. "Thanks, Joe. What're you having?"

"An éclair and plain old coffee." Joe told the owner behind the counter and Dana at the same time. "Did you get the lady's order?"

Bonnie blinked at Joe in stupefied silence.

"Tiramisu and espresso, Bonnie." Dana reminded her gently.

"Sure, that'll be $17.00 please. We'll bring it to you." Sara, Bonnie's sister and partner, answered for her.

Dana laughed, soft and low, as they chose a table close to the wall.

"What?"

"Do women always lose their ability to speak around you?"

He flushed. He hated questions like that.

"I withdraw the question." Who knew his face could turn that shade of red under his tan?

Joe grunted.

Steaming cups arrived with delicate plates of desserts and silver forks.

"This is a nice place." Joe forked up his first bite of éclair. "Mmmm."

Dana watched his eyes close in appreciation and the satisfied smile light his face with her expert eyes. She could smell the fresh, eggy pastry and deep chocolate coating. The scent of her own dessert drew her to taste it.

The sensations crossed her tongue, the hazelnut, the moist cake, the rich cream, and the dusting of espresso powder on top. "Mmmm," she echoed Joe.

"This is good, Dana. I've been running around like crazy for weeks. Sitting still feels good."

Eyes on his while he spoke, Dana saw something in them. A hot and steamy tryst starring the two of them. Mesmerized by the sight, she reached for her espresso. Looking down into her cup gave her a break from what they were both thinking about now. So it's like that, is it, Dana thought.

"It's nice to get away from my kitchen and eat something somebody else made. Thank you." She went for a casual tone, one that said she wasn't about to become a notch in anyone's belt, nice guy or no.

"How did you get started writing cookbooks?

Carter told me that's why we're getting those great meals."

"When my husband passed away I decided to take a course in catering. Everyone said I was a great cook and I loved it so I thought it was a good way for me to earn a living and be home a lot with Jason and Jenny.

Four years into it I catered a very fancy bridal shower and one of the guests happened to be a cookbook editor. She sought me out in the kitchen and asked if I'd like to do a book."

Dana couldn't see the way her whole body lit up when she told her story, but she could see the way Joe pressed back into his chair, impressed by her passion for her work.

"That's a great story." Joe finished his coffee and couldn't stifle the yawn that slipped out.

They laughed together.

"Shall we?" Dana pointed at the door.

"Yeah, I keep a very exciting schedule these days. I work from before dawn until dusk."

"I'll see you tomorrow. I have all new stuff for you guys to try."

"So this is every week?"

"Almost every week."

"Great. Drive safe. I'll be by around six if that's okay?"

"That's prefect if you want to get there when the

guys are back from practice."

"I appreciate Jason giving Carter a ride home from practice. Is it alright with you if I offer him some gas money?"

Dana considered. "Sure you can, but I don't think he'll take it."

"Why not?"

"Because like me he won't think he's gone too much out of his way for Carter."

"Hmm. That's very nice of you two."

She shrugged. "See you tomorrow, Joe."

Chapter 4

"What, what, what, what, what, what, what, what, what, what, what, what, what."

Dana's mind rose slowly from oblivion to confusion.

"Why, why, why, why, why, why, why, why, why, why, why, why."

"No, no, no, no, no, no, no, no, no."

She opened one eye, testing.

There he was, on the hover board.

"Hello," Dana greeted.

"How, how, how, how, how, how, how, how, how, how, how, how, how."

Dana glanced around, looking for the source of the voice. The man on the hover board floated, unblinking.

"What is your name?" She thought that since he figured so prominently in all of her weird dreams lately she might as well know something about him.

"You," he answered.

"When, when, when, when, when, when, when,

when, when, when, when, when, when," the faceless voice continued.

She turned her head to where it seemed to be coming from and found nothing there. She turned back to You. "I'm Dana." She sat up in her bed.

"I know."

"That's handy." Dana walked to her living room, curious to see what You did.

He followed her. And this was not her living room.

A group of horses munched on bales of dried grass in front of her. In the distance she saw a gorgeous house. Joe stood on the front porch.

She felt sand beneath her bare feet. Glancing down, she was pleased to see that her toenails were painted a flattering shade of pink.

Joe waved at them from the porch, welcoming them. You followed silently behind.

The night was warm and soft around them. Crickets chirped a constant song.

"Dana, You, welcome." Joe pointed to a porch swing. "Would either of you like to sit down?"

"You know You?" She tried to make the question sound better in her mind than it did to her ears.

"Yes, I do. I see that you have also met You. I thought you had but it didn't seem the thing to ask so soon." He sat on a chair across from her.

She was suddenly aware of her skimpy t-shirt and shorts.

"No need to worry, Dana. You're gorgeous here and there."

"You know what I'm thinking?" The thought was frightening.

"When you spend time in The Dreaming you start to pick up on things. You know, not everyone can come here." Joe's chair turned into a recliner that he leaned back in, very much at home.

"I actually don't know very much about this at all."

"I'll be honest, Dana, I'm thrilled to meet you here and in The World. Very few people I meet here have a presence in The World and vice versa."

He waved a hand and a table appeared between them, bearing coffee and chocolates.

She reached for a chocolate and found her hand on the pillow beside the one she was laying on. Some dream, she thought, not even one bite of chocolate.

Joe knocked on the front door, nervous and excited.

She opened the door to him, smiling and wondering if she should mention the dream.

He took the irrevocable step of holding out a box of See's chocolates. "You left before you got a piece."

She was completely stunned.

Chapter 5

"I know. Sit down?"

She stared at him, numbly sitting on her favorite reading couch.

"Want one?" He offered the box.

She wasn't the first woman he'd met in The Dreaming and in The World, she was the third. The other two had promptly disappeared from The Dreaming, and from his life, after he told them he knew about the shared dreams.

She remembered the voice from the night before, how it had repeated what, why, no, and how. She heard the same rhythmic cadence in her head now.

She shook her head mutely.

"I've been in The Dreaming all my life. I saw that this was your third visit. I hope you'll forgive me for investigating you after you left. Seeing you there was a little bit of a shock even though I suspected you had been there." He shifted on the chair, not sure what to do with the box of chocolates.

Dana found a solid thought to hold onto. "You could read my mind there."

"I'll do my best not to read it here, now," Joe promised.

She felt vulnerable, naked.

He sent a thought her way, testing. *"It can work both ways."*

Her eyes widened in surprise, and then even more surprising for her was the euphoria that flooded her. *"It...does. It's a little scary."*

He smiled calmly, enjoying the emotions she was feeling. Who knew how long they would last?

"Dad, there's a whole table full of food in here. I've never tasted chicken and dumplings like this before!" Carter called out to him from the dining room.

"Can Carter?" She tentatively thought to Joe, still testing.

"No," he answered.

"I love this...I think. I'm a little confused." Dana laughed to herself.

He chuckled out loud. "I'm ready to taste those chicken and dumplings. It's a long time favorite of mine and Carter's."

As she and Joe walked to the dining room she "saw" him experience memories that had happened there, including the phone call telling her about Ben's heart attack.

The Dreaming

"How do you live with that? There's so much stuff in your head!" She handed Joe a plate.

"I got used to it. I've been able to do this my entire life." He walked around the table, scooping up creamed corn, chicken and dumplings, maple carrots, biscuits, green bean casserole, and garlic mushrooms. "How long did it take you to make all of this?"

"Pretty much the whole day. That's why I do it once a week. I don't cook a lot on other days."

"Yeah, she does. It's a good thing her food is healthy or we would weigh 300 pounds." Jason picked up another biscuit and piled it high with green bean casserole for his own sandwich. No plate. No fork. Perfect.

"It's a good thing I tasted the food last week *before* I heard it was healthy." Joe tried to hold back the shudder that went through him.

"You have an interesting impression of health promoting food, Joe." Her expression teased and censored so artfully he felt only mildly chastised for his rightful hesitation. What people would eat instead of good tasting food in the name of living longer and looking better baffled him.

Jenny came in through the garage then, obviously upset.

She *looked* great in her jeans and shirt declaring PEACE in matching tie-dyed blues and purples.

Her hair was up in a pony tail. Her make-up smeared from crying.

Jenny looked at Joe, Jeremy, Jason, Carter, and Dana, sniffling as she exited the room with a muffled, teary, "Hi, guys."

"I'll be back," Dana followed her, adjusting what she had just learned from Joe, the enormity of it, with the surprise of a dramatic moment, and her normal Wednesday routine.

Dana walked from the dining room to the hallway carpeted in soft, deep plush, blue carpet. She loved the color she had chosen to match the blue of her twin's eyes. Someday in the not too far future they would be gone, living in their own apartments. She'd still have this wonderful house filled with their memories. The cream colored walls bordered in blue roses. She thought of her home as sweet, cozy, and warm.

She tapped on Jenny's closed door. "It's mom, honey, can I come in?" She laid her face against the door to wait for the response. It felt cool under her cheek.

"Yes."

Dana sat on the bed with Jenny and opened her arms to her. Jenny nuzzled into her mom's neck and brought her breathing under control.

Dana knew that waiting for her to talk was best. They sat that way, holding each other on the soft

The Dreaming

pink bedspread, leaning against the pillows.

"He's going out with Sally. He's all over her, and it sucks. It makes me so mad. We went out for two months and he barely even came to school. Now I see him and her kissing all over each other and today, TODAY, he acted like I wasn't even there!" Jenny's words rushed out in one long breath while she cleaned her face with the tissue Dana pulled from the dispenser on the nightstand.

"That couldn't have been easy for you." Dana took the empathetic route. She reasoned out that the "he" in question hadn't treated Jenny very well at all. He had taught her the painful lesson of actually dating one of the troubled bad boys at her high school instead of stopping at giggling about what she and her friends thought he was like. They had ended the mystery with the awareness that he was flaky.

Jenny sobbed some more into her mother's shoulder and then straightened. Her mood shifted like lightening. "Jim said he wants to go to Disneyland for our anniversary." She beamed a smile brighter than the sun at Dana.

The parts of Dana that were entertained by the little play Jenny had just treated her to stayed inside of her. No need to invite whatever Jenny would react with if she shared her mirth.

"So many possibilities...let's start with dinner. I hope you're at least a little hungry?" She rubbed an encouraging hand over Jenny's back.

"What's the dessert?"

"Blueberry-peach cobbler and homemade vanilla bean ice cream."

Jenny was in the dining room figuring out how much she had to eat before her mom would let her have dessert by the time the word "vanilla" passed her lips.

"I smell chocolate." Jenny sniffed the air.

"There is also a chocolate fudge center cake."

Every head in the room turned in her direction.

"I'd say the name of the recipe is working for you." She smiled at the group of faces in front of her.

Chapter 6

"Hello?"

"Hello, Joe? It's Dana. I wondered if I could ask you a question?" She played nervously with the phone cord.

"Sure."

"Why does You limit the number of questions I'm allowed to ask him in my dreams?" She had debated calling but she really wanted to know. Okay, she also wanted to talk with Joe.

"Hmmm. I would tell you to ask him but I can understand why you're asking me." He settled back in his chair, considering. "Could you meet me in The Dreaming tonight?"

"How do I get it to happen? From what I can tell it happens when it wants to."

"Do you have dreams that are not in The Dreaming?" His curiosity perked up.

"Oh, wow. Not anymore. Not since..." Dana calculated in her head, "Not since the night before I met you."

Joe's silence was so profound Dana felt it loud and clear.

"I don't know how much to tell you about a vision they brought me five years ago. Man, it's already been five years." He mused, distracted.

"Joe, what vision?" She felt that same combination of anxious euphoria she had felt on Wednesday when he told her that they were so vividly in each other's dreams.

Dana felt him struggle with his thoughts and feelings. She felt his clarity when he made his choice.

"I was told that there would be a special woman for me and Carter someday in the future. They said she would discover The Dreaming when I met her." He sighed raggedly, not liking how it sounded coming out of his mouth. Afraid of what it sounded like to her.

She took the same path Joe had, sorting through her thoughts and feelings. To his credit, he was obviously sensitive to how fantastic this sounded to her.

"Dana, I don't expect anything to happen between us because of the vision. It shows a woman, but it could be a different woman." That didn't come out right, damn it. "What I mean is...I..."

She laughed nervously.

The Dreaming

The awkward silence pounded loudly between them.

She broke the tension. "I guess since I only dream in The Dreaming I can meet you there. How's that?"

He sighed gratefully. "I'll ask You about your limit on your questions when we're there together. That's new for me."

She let out a big breath and went for the question that she really wanted the answer to. "Joe, are the visions always right?" She didn't know what she wanted the answer to be.

"Always."

Chapter 7

Dana relaxed with extreme pleasure. She held in her hands a ticket to paradise. Beside her, on the adorable decoupage tea table was a steaming earthenware mug of hazelnut coffee flavored with delicious cream.

She laid back on her favorite reading couch and dove into the story. The story wove into her, taking her inside it. She cared for the characters, feeling her own emotions respond when they struggled with the challenges they faced.

The story in her hands, so well crafted, mirrored the intense experience she was having, and made her even more grateful for what she wasn't having. Joe was...what? One of a kind.

She had made a lot out of her life. She started out with a good middle class childhood. Her parents, god love them, had always done whatever they deemed "right" where she was concerned. That had included encouraging her to marry Ben Carapelli. It was such a "smart" match.

She sipped the coffee, held the book, and reflected on how "smart" and "good" could be so far apart.

She had felt the wonderful feelings she read about for Ben for about a hot second of the years they had spent together.

She could have left, she supposed. It would have meant risking her parents censor. She was educated, just as Ben had been. She could have supported herself and the twins easily.

For a time they were seen as a power couple. They dated all through college. She got her degree in nutrition, he became a lawyer. Still, in time, she had come to see that their rigidly "smart" courtship and marriage lacked more than just the difference between what a starry eyed girl who loved romance from as far back as she could remember could dream about and what everyday people shared.

Had he loved her? Had she loved him? She hugged herself as she breathed out a sigh of the old heartache.

The moment pulled her back to her living room then. She was taking a couple of hours off of her busy schedule to indulge, not to feel sad about what had been.

She was a long way away from Dana, Ben's stay home wife and the mother of his kids who gave the awesome client dinner and welcomed the so-so sex life they had shared.

She was a successful business woman, a loving mother, a published, and, pinch, famous cookbook author.

She lifted the book again and immersed herself in the old time country kitchen in the story.

As she read she thought of that nagging, elusive key to making that garlic mushroom gravy work with her dumplings. The dumplings were great. The garlic mushrooms were great. She licked the plate clean of the sauce when she made it and it was very healthy. She could make it work once she found that one thing that made it click.

Her mind drifted to the apple cinnamon stuffed pancakes she was trying to bring to life. How thick should she make them? How much apple cinnamon filling should there be in each pancake? She puzzled and concluded as she noted her ideas on the lined pad of paper she kept near her most of the time.

She tasted, measured, smelled, and computed to what seemed to be the best starting point to start working on it in the kitchen when the time came.

Her creative surge satisfied, she reached again for the coffee and the poignant love story.

"So, Dana, what's new?" Lucy held her question for as long as it took the waiter to take two steps away from the table. Her friend since forever could see that there was something very different about her pal Dana.

"I don't even know where to begin." She laughed and sipped from her wine glass. The wine was meant to pair with the endive appetizer that was her first course.

"Just start at the very beginning, the very best place to start." Lucy sang the lyric from Do-Re-Mi.

"Ha. Ha. Ha." Dana smiled.

Their lunches were a combination of work and play. Two nutritionists that were now a cookbook author and a restaurant critic brought a lot of perspective to the "What Lucy thinks about..." column.

"The plating is bland for foodies, but lovely for a special lunch out," Dana observed.

"Hmm. The prices are high enough for better plating for anyone." Lucy disagreed.

The restaurant hadn't been reviewed in quite some time and, delightfully, they didn't seem to know who Lucy was.

The restaurant seated 200. The menu was French Nouveau. The executive chef was known for thinking just a touch more highly of himself than his performance warranted.

"It's decent. I'm not impressed. Predictable might be the word for our meal here." Lucy pushed her plate away, signaling that she was done with her course.

"We ordered French onion soup and they're the predictable ones?"

"Clever, Dana, so clever." Lucy tried for annoyed, almost made it. "So what's going on, something with the kids? Ooooh, oooh, oooh, is it a man? Please tell me it's a man." Lucy was clapping her hands in excitement and bouncing around on her seat.

"The most obvious thing that's going on is that I've been having some really strange dreams. They're lucid, like usual for me, but they're different than everything I've had before." She fiddled with her silverware. "There was a man I know in the last one. The strangest part about that is that he knew he was in the dream." She left off the part about being telepathic with him. She was still trying to handle that one herself. She felt like she might be just a little over the edge there. Maybe the publication pressure was getting to her and she hadn't noticed?

"Are you having sexy dreams with this guy? Please tell me you're having sexy dreams with him. Is he cute?"

She caught Lucy's good mood right then.

Maybe she could have some fun with this.

"Or is he giving you funny brownies and cookies?" Concern passed over Lucy's face.

"We went out for coffee and dessert, he didn't

The Dreaming

make those, and he gave me See's candies after the dream. No, I don't think it's that, but thanks for putting that in my head."

The waiter, Henry, brought gorgeous bowls of French onion soup. The toasted cheese bread laid perfectly, artfully, on top.

"Mmmm." Dana enjoyed the scent of the fragrant broth rising up from the bowl.

"It does smell good." Lucy flipped the topic back. "Are you feeding him?"

"He's been over the last two Wednesdays. His son is on the track team with Jason, so when he came to pick Carter up that first time I offered dinner. You know I like to have a lot of people there in the testing stages."

"But he took you out and bought you chocolates?" Lucy tasted the bread and graded it as above average.

"The part that bugs me is these dreams. The dogs were talking to me in the second one and they seem different to me now, more involved in my life in some weird way. Like they know things and are telling me about them." She shuddered delicately with the thought.

The look on Peach's face the other day, sort of a knowing grin, surfaced in her memory for Dana to look at right at that moment.

"Back to the guy...he knew he was in your dream? How did you find that out? What's his name?"

"Wait a sec. This bread is fantastic and the broth, for once, isn't too salty. I've got hope for my salmon en croute."

"You're avoiding, D." Lucy tried for annoyed again but her bouncy personality didn't stretch there.

"The way he showed me that he was in my dream was...creative." Dana's face took on a new, dreamy look that Lucy hadn't seen before.

"Uh oh."

"His name is Joe and yes, he's good looking. He's actually really good looking."

From the corner of her eye Dana saw a flash, like a little bright light and quick movement. It reminded her of You somehow. When she turned her head there was nothing there.

"You're feeding him, D, please don't get too attached just yet. You know what I mean?" Lucy laid a protective hand over Dana's. She was the veteran of many sad endings, and she saw a vulnerability on her friend's face that worried her.

"You're a great friend, Luce. Who would've thought we'd be sitting here, eating this rich food, having this conversation. Only you and I could pull this off."

"And neither of us has to get the check. I love my job."

"*I* love your job, too. So, do they get some credit for the soup? Have a heart, that's damn good bread."

The Dreaming

Dana argued for the soup in her friendly, passionate way.

"Yeah, they do, and if they can impress either of us with the salmon en croute we'll be looking at some nice words in their favor. The wait staff is good."

"I like the chairs and the art on the walls, too. Have you checked the bathroom? If Jenny was with us she would have told us what scent the bathroom soap is by now."

They laughed together over her daughter's fondness for bathrooms and scented soap.

Dana felt better after their time together. Lucy didn't seem at all concerned about her weird dreams and she knew her advice where Joe was concerned was good. Their lunch, all in all, was above average. She counted the day as a success.

Chapter 8

"Dana?" Joe stood at the fence in his yard and thought her way. He'd discovered, by looking in the books, that they would meet in The Dreaming that night when they slept. He was testing to see if their telepathy was as good from a distance as it had been when they were face to face.

He wasn't letting himself get excited about Dana and the obvious connection they were sharing. He knew, too well, that not everyone could accept all that he knew. All that he could do.

Carter's mother had been annoyed by it, especially when it made it as plain as the nose on his face that her claims of "working late" were actually her getting naked with her boss.

They had parted ways then, divorcing as amiably as Joe could make it for Carter. Her thoughts were more on her new life as the girlfriend of a rich man.

For a time he and Carter had stayed on the ranch they had brought Carter home from the hospital to,

The Dreaming

so that Carter could be close to his mother.

It became obvious, and painful, for both of them when that didn't encourage her to be a part of Carter's world.

He'd heard about this ranch, the one he stood on now, through some friends of his that wanted to sell after owning for so long. They wanted to travel, not to tend stock every day. Joe had judged it as a good opportunity to start over in a fresh spot.

It was an upgrade for him, a sign of his own success that he'd made enough over the years to buy a bigger spread. The stables here were well established, and he had purchased them along with the land, the house, the buildings, and some of the best breeding stock in the business.

It was a shame that Beth wasn't there for Carter. But he was. Solid.

"Joe?" Dana sat in her bathtub, grateful the bubbles were covering her. For all she knew, he could see her.

She heard him chuckle. She would bet money that he was smiling.

"I thought it was a good idea to see if you could hear me from a distance." He walked up to the porch to sit while they talked.

"This saves on the phone bill. It's as private as you can get, too." She settled back into the tub, feeling relaxed and enjoying the novelty.

"I, uh, can't see you in any clear way. I get something like the impression of what you're doing. I can hear you thinking." He thought it was only fair that she know that.

She sighed. This smacked of intimacy and she wasn't sure what that meant for her. She'd kept things light when it came to men since Ben's death. She didn't think she was going to be able to keep this quite as light. She didn't know yet if she wanted to or not.

"So now we've got the test results. I appreciate your candor in telling me that you can hear my thoughts. I think it sits better with me to know."

"I do everything I can not to invade your privacy, Dana. That's not what I'm after."

Her next thought was clear to both of them. What was he after?

"Thank you, Joe. I know you mean that."

He smiled, pleased that she knew he was sincere. It was possible, just possible, that she was going to be able to read him as clearly, so now was as good a time as any to get used to being open with one another.

"The reason for my, um, contacting you is that I see that we'll be together in The Dreaming tonight. I wanted to give you a heads up."

She took a moment to think about how she felt about that. *"How do you know ahead of time?"*

"There are books there that I can look in for

information. I took a look to see if I could find out when we'd see one another there again."

Her interest peaked. She hadn't known Joe very long, that was true, but somehow she knew that this was an adventure and not a nightmare. One that they somehow shared.

"Well, then, I appreciate you taking time to tell me so that I'll be ready. I have a lot of questions and so far I've been limited in what I could do with them. Having a guide is really helpful."

Classy. Polite. Sincere. Smart. Hot. Funny. Whatcha gonna do, Joe, with a woman like that? He was looking forward to finding out. If she was interested, that is.

"I can imagine how confusing it would be. I hardly remember myself, since the first time I realized that everyone wasn't visiting The Dreaming I was about 16 years old. No one ever talked about it and I wondered why. I found out it was because they didn't know about it."

"Thanks again. Since you'll be my tour guide I suppose I won't have to rely on You's limited information tonight."

"It doesn't look that way." He hesitated, knowing that he should tell her what he was thinking about was possible for them. He sensed he could easily scare her off. He also knew that she wouldn't play games with him and so he wasn't about to play them

with her.

He took the plunge.

"Dana, as to what I'm after...the sky's the limit there. I like you. I like your kids. I'd like to take you to dinner and just keep on seeing where it goes. How does that sit with you?"

Her lips curved up in a feline smile she swore she had never smiled before. There was something about him that made her feel electric. Desirable.

"It sits fine with me, Joe. Going to dinner with you sounds like fun. Seeing where it goes sounds," she sighed, *"like just the thing for us."*

He breathed easier hearing her, sensing her. She was so polite he hadn't been sure she was interested in him beyond the fact that he was Carter's dad.

"I'd like to take you to dinner, then, tomorrow night? I'd appreciate it if you pick the place since I don't know them. I could pick you up at 7:00?"

"There's a place, a little bit of a drive, but the food is dynamite. Do you like Indian?"

"What I've tried, I've liked. I don't mind the drive, either. We haven't seen much since we've been here."

"So we're set?"

He sensed her distraction and ended by telling her they were set and he'd see her later.

Chapter 9

Huge statues of the number 4 surrounded her. She walked to the closest one, glanced around, counting 25 of them close by and more in the distance trailing off as they were further and further away.

Dana reached out to the four in front of her and felt it smooth and solid beneath her fingertips. Her conscious mind picked up on it then, that she was in The Dreaming.

You glided down to her on his hover board.

"Good evening, You."

"Good evening, Dana."

It seemed reasonable to use a question to ask how to get to Joe.

"Can you show me where Joe is?"

"I'm here, Dana." Joe came from her left, rounding one of the gigantic number 4's. "Hello, You."

"Joe, it's a pleasure to see you." You was as expressionless as ever. His tone flat, as always.

"What's with all the 4's?" Joe asked her. He was

dressed in a pair of sweat pants and a t-shirt. The white of it flattered his tan and his dark hair.

"I don't know." She glanced down and saw that the sleeping shorts and tank she had chosen to fall asleep in, in the hope that they were what she would be in here, were indeed on her. That relaxed her. A little.

The kiss, he thought. Man, we should just get that over with. See what the spark is like.

Dana touched her fingers to her lips, surprised that they were tingling. She looked at Joe then and saw his thought clearly. That would explain the tingle. So if he thinks about a kiss and my lips tingle, what would happen if I thought about what he looks like without the sweats? She felt slightly wicked with it, and with the knowledge that there was at least a chance he would know exactly what she was thinking.

He turned to face You, but not before she saw the bulge in his sweats. Holy moly, a thought had given him a hard-on.

The fantasy of it was too hard to resist. She knew Joe, knew that they were already close to intimate. She deliberately imagined sliding her hand over his ass.

"Is that an offer? I am only human you know." Joe tried for casual. He'd imagined much more when they were drinking coffee so he really couldn't hold

The Dreaming

it against her.

"It worked." Her voice held the wonder she felt.

"Listen, Dana, The Dreaming and The World are connected. Sometimes I see things here that I later see in The World and vice versa. This is still, somehow, real. What we do here affects our emotions and our bodies." His eyes lingered over her breasts as he spoke the word "bodies."

Her nipples pearled and poked through her tank top.

Dana turned to You, hovering there, looking at nothing. Still she knew that he was completely aware of what took place between her and Joe.

"I apologize if I'm coming off as a tease." Dana walked to him then, picked up his hand. In their time together there had been very little touching. None of it initiated by her.

"Trust me when I say that this is new for both of us." He laced his fingers with hers, lifted it, kissed her skin. He smiled into her eyes.

Enchanted, Dana reached up to kiss his lips. It was a gentle, friendly kiss. It shouldn't have flashed fire through her and started a throb between her legs. It shouldn't have made her sigh with the sweetness of the way he moved his lips over hers.

"The feeling is mutual." He raised his free hand to the back of her head, stroking her silky brown hair with the palm of his hand.

* * *

"Mom, mom, mooooom." Jenny stared at her mother, concerned when she didn't get a response.

Dana sat at the kitchen table, a breakfast quiche in front of her that she was testing for quality after freezing and reheating. Her coffee cup was in her hand, her fingers registering the heat of the liquid through it.

"Yes, Jenny, sorry." Dana shook herself out of it.

"What's up with you? You look like you're in another world." Jenny forked a bite of banana pancake to her lips, another one of the frozen experiments. She made a happy hum at the taste of it.

Dana observed the reaction to the pancake and was happy to know that it was passing the test. It seemed that a lot of things were going right for her.

"I'm distracted, I admit it. I have a date tonight. I'm already thinking about what to wear." Dana smiled at that, at the simple connecting that she and Jenny did this way.

"With who?" Jason was munching down his third bowl of whole wheat cereal with unsweetened rice milk. She was very lucky with him. He had hardly ever complained about the absence of sugar cereal in their house.

The Dreaming

"Joe." She was looking for reactions. She knew she was already *in* something with him, whatever it was it would not only be unfair to hide from the kids, but impossible. They would find it out anyway.

Jason looked a little surprised. Not Jenny. Jenny looked happy.

"Joe, Carter's dad, Joe?" Jason looked like he was trying to figure it out. Did Carter's dad want to nail his mom? Ewww. Better not go there.

"That would be him." Dana smiled at them both, glad to be sharing a quiet breakfast together.

"Sweeeet," Jenny beamed at her mom as she bounced up to rinse her dishes and put them in the dishwasher.

"So, what's the point of that?" Jason asked. He wasn't done with it yet. What did she want from it?

"Dinner, conversation." Dana blushed a little, thinking of the dream kiss. And the dream that had ended before she learned anything new about the fascinating new place Joe called The Dreaming.

"Hmmm. So do you two have like, a thing going? Like Carter could be my stepbrother type of thing?"

"It's too early for anyone to be thinking like that. We're going out to eat, we like each other. It is a date, we're not just friends." She placed her hand on Jason's, briefly.

"Sweeet. Well I don't care what time you get home. Go crazy, mom. He's hot."

Dana laughed. "I can't say the same for you. Mind yourself, young lady. I'll have my cell on me if anybody needs anything."

"Is it alright if Carter hangs here while you go out? We were planning on watching 'The Texas Chainsaw Massacre' marathon."

"Yes, but no one else unless you clear it with me first. If you go out, I want to know about it." Dana had her mom voice on, the you-know-what-I-expect-and-I-expect-a lot, voice.

"Sheesh, mom, what do you think we're gonna do? Hire a couple of hookers and get some e?"

New, truly uncomfortable thoughts cycled through her mind. "It hadn't crossed my mind. Thanks for putting *that* in my head."

"I'm here tonight, too, mom. Cat's coming over and we're gonna do some karaoke, stuff like that."

Dana considered and felt good about the combination of teens that would be here on their own while she had a night out with Joe.

"Sounds like a good Friday night to me. House rules. You know 'em. You love 'em. I expect you to follow 'em."

Eye rolls and doors slamming were the grateful response.

Chapter 10

Joe and Carter arrived together at 7:00. Peaches and Cream announced their arrival and enthusiastically welcomed them in when Jason opened the door to them.

Dana had chosen a dress for their date. She wore pants and shorts all the time, so dressing up and feeling female for a change had made her nerves disappear.

The dress was sexy. She had accepted that her attraction to Joe was very sexual and she didn't feel the need to shy away from it as she had on other dates. She knew he wanted her. He looked at her with more than the typical man appreciation and she had seen it in his eyes.

Her green eyes were played up with lush dark lashes. She had blushed her cheeks and lips a soft pink. Her skin was smoothly polished and scented with her favorite Bath & Body Works scent, Moonlight Path.

She could admit with complete humility that she looked stunning.

"Since this is the first time you're going to be here when I'm not, Carter, I'm going over the house rules with you. You can eat or drink anything in the house that you and your dad already agree on. If you have a question, text me. My number's on the fridge, and Jason has it, of course. You, Jason, Jenny, and Cat have free run of the house, but you may not have anyone else here without clearing it with me first. If you decide to go out, you need to clear it ahead of time. Questions?"

Carter decided that this thing could be cool, his dad going out with Mrs. C.

"No, no questions, Mrs. C. We're cool here. I already ate, but I bet I can handle some snacks while we watch the movies." He said it casually, like he wasn't already thinking of the possibilities of raiding the fridge.

"Are we ready, Joe? Do you have anything else to add?"

She didn't see it, but they stood together while she addressed the teens. It was natural for her to stand with him that way, as a unit. It felt natural for everyone watching.

"Yeah, if you don't mind, I'd like to add that the guys need to respect the girls. Watch your volume, knock before you enter a room, no burping contests, keep your pants on instead of stripping down to your boxers. Clear?"

Jason laughed out loud but remembered at that moment that Carter didn't have a sister so he may not have thought of that kind of stuff.

Dana nodded to Joe, impressed. "Good thinking."

"Right, we're out. We both have cell phones so let us know if you need us."

Joe held the door for her, holding his gaze at the back of her head as she stepped in front of him when he really wanted to check out her legs and her walk in the short, body hugging black dress.

He already felt like he had a neon sign painted on him that he was hot for her.

He hadn't brought many women around Carter, and there was a reason for that. He wouldn't encourage Carter to get close unless he thought something could last. He already knew she was a classy woman or they wouldn't have gotten this far.

Door closed behind them, Dana felt Joe's eyes on her. She sensed that his thoughts were on her, also, and that they were intense.

She moved ahead of him on the walk to his truck, which she noticed was shiny as always.

"Do you think they're watching?" Joe wanted that kiss. He didn't see why they should wait until the end of the night.

"I don't suppose it matters if they are or not.

We'll just keep it to PG-13 if you're wanting to kiss hello."

"You smell incredible. It matches how you look." Joe opened her door for her.

"Thank you. I've never seen you look anything but good, but I have to say those slacks and that shirt look amazing on you."

"What about the cologne? Do you like it?" He was flirting. He was fishing. He was panting.

They stood there, she on the seat with her legs crossed, facing him, the long smooth of her legs ending in strappy black heels. He had one hand on the door, the other on the top of the truck, caging her in.

She leaned forward a little, aware that her full breasts were a focal point for both of them. She wore a short silver necklace with an emerald solitaire at the center. She sniffed. "I do like it, Joe, you have good taste."

He closed in then, his hands safely on the truck, and teased her lips open with his. She responded, smiling into his mouth, savoring the moment of their first, or was it second, kiss?

"So, I'm in for a treat, hmm?" Joe spoke against her lips. He pulled back to round the truck and get them to the restaurant. He was starving.

* * *

The Dreaming

Her cheeks hurt from laughing, from smiling.

When had she ever felt this free with a man? The simple answer was, never.

"Is it scaring you?" Joe drove away from the club they had slipped into for dancing after dinner.

"What?" She was sitting on the seat next to him, legs gathered under her and turned to the side to face Joe.

"What's happening here. We met, what, a month ago?"

"Hmmm." She considered. He looked straight ahead, his face gave nothing away. "In some ways. You?"

"In some ways. I've been out of the dating thing for so long, I don't know what to do about it. Ideas?" His arm rested across the bench, his hand on her shoulder. It felt good there.

"Well, if you had a good time tonight then I would think that you should ask me to do it again sometime. If I had a good time I'll say yes. Thoughts?"

He chuckled, liking the easiness of it. "You mean you think we could do that, simple like that?"

She thought of the way they had danced together, the way they had nearly sat in each other's laps at dinner, eating from the same plates and forks. Drinking from the same glasses. Feeding each other. It had been simple. And she was already frustrated that she knew she wouldn't take her clothes off for him just yet. She had to know him better. Still, there was something between that and a kiss goodnight at her door.

"To a degree," she answered.

They were in their city now, a few blocks away from her house and their kids. Joe pulled into the parking lot of the closed post office.

"I'm not looking just to get laid here. You know that, right?"

She knew. The moment he put the truck in park she slid closer, to feel that incredible connection they shared, soft and electric at the same time.

They had shared many kisses already tonight. They had held each other close while they danced, her heels bringing their lips almost even.

His hands hadn't strayed below her waist or into her top. He had kissed her neck, her face, her hands. Her shoulders. But it was all with respect.

"Isn't that the classic line for a situation just like this?" she teased.

"How do I know you're not just looking for sex?" Joe put both arms around her and asked the question in her ear.

"I guess you don't," she flirted back.

"I like you. I had a good time tonight. Can I take you out again sometime? There's a picnic next Saturday. One of my boarders is celebrating an anniversary and having a big deal at their place.

The Dreaming

We'll bring the kids. If you like."

"I don't know their schedules, but if they're around I'll invite them to go with us."

"So it's a date, then?"

"Umm hmm. Are you coming over Wednesday for testing? Normal time?"

"Yep. I think that works for me. So, we'll be seeing a lot of each other. In The World and most likely in The Dreaming."

"Umm hmm." She opened deep to the kiss, feeling them blend in yet another unmistakable, indefinable way.

"While we're exploring this I'd like to know if there's anyone else? If you're dating anyone else?" They were cuddled together, snug and warm.

"No."

"I'm going out on a limb here and say that I'd prefer it if we didn't see anyone else until we know what we've got here. I don't think it's fair to these hypothetical people to go on a date thinking they might have a shot when it's this intense between us already." That beat it, right there. This was not an opinion he had ever felt a need for on the first official date. But they had said he wouldn't be able to mistake this for anything less than what it was.

Dana pulled back, looked into his eyes. It wasn't really any big deal to agree to that since she didn't date much anyway and there wasn't anyone else she wanted to date.

They moved to each other for their good night kiss and this time she let her hands roam around his chest, his face, his biceps. She moaned into his mouth when he gripped her ass, running his hands over it.

He was the one to pull back. "I'm already going to have enough trouble sleeping tonight without going any further."

She smiled, and felt that feline purring inside of her again. "I've got a question, really just a curiosity. Is it possible for us to be...together...in The Dreaming?"

"We'd have to ditch You before we could do that. I can see him hovering there, but yeah, I think it's possible."

Joe vibrated his excitement when he burst out, "Shit, I just saw it. Look at this, remember all the 4's last time we were in The Dreaming together? Today is the 4th, my odometer reading is 44,444 miles, and I remember seeing more 4's on the bill at the restaurant." He took out the receipt and confirmed. "It was $44.00 with everything. By the way, that was a very good meal for what they charge. We should go back."

She beamed a smile his way. "We should."

As she laid down in bed she looked over the night in her memory. It had been carefree, it had been delicious,

The Dreaming

it had been safe and sexy. And the 4's, she couldn't get a grasp on all the 4's. She felt giddy.

"Dana."

"Hmmm?"

"Good night."

"Good night, Joe."

"Can you make those lentils, like the ones we had tonight?"

"Umm hmm. The book came out a couple of years ago. It's called 'Dana Cooks Indian Food.'"

"So I won't be tasting any of that on Wednesday?" The tastes of the evening were still filling his mind. Maybe there was something addictive in those spices.

"Hmm, no, the testing's just about done."

The yawn that came across to Joe was sweet and compellingly sexy. He laughed at himself. He knew he had it bad when he was moved by a yawn.

"We both need to get some sleep. Tomorrow's already started." He was torn. Part of him wanted to stay up all night talking with her, the other wanted her to sleep and be refreshed for her day.

The reluctance they felt to part was clear to both of them.

"Dana, one last thing before we say good night for real. I found some more 4's. I'm 44."

"Really? I wondered. I'm not very good at pinning down how old someone is. I'm seeing what you mean about The Dreaming showing up in The

World. I have more to tell you on that, too."

She was nearly asleep, her words were slow and breathy with it.

"Great. Night, Dana."

She cuddled into her pillow, happy she felt like he was right there with her.

Chapter 11

Dana pulled up to the curb at her house, curious to see her driveway crowded with Joe, Carter, and Jason bending over the open hood of Jason's car.

"Problem?" She asked as she walked to them with a canvas shopping bag of groceries slung over her shoulder.

Joe felt that calm warmth that somehow managed to flash with excited lust as he watched her walk toward him. If he was more poetic he might tell her that she carried spring sunshine with her all the time, soft and fresh and bright.

"Minor," Joe answered. "Carter mentioned that he thought he heard a noise when they were riding home the other day so I thought I'd take a look. It's something we can handle ourselves."

He looked like Mr. Handy, she thought, in his jeans and t-shirt. He looked right at home there, as he seemed to everywhere she saw him.

"Thanks. I like knowing it's being kept up. That's

part of the deal, right, Jase?"

"Uh huh." He was glad it wasn't going to cost a lot. The deal was that his mom would help with repairs only when he didn't have the cash to do it himself, and that was very conditional depending on whether he could reasonably have had that amount of money set aside for "unexpected expenses." If he didn't have a car for awhile, oh well. If he didn't do the preventive maintenance and it caused a problem, oh well.

Dana thought about a kiss hello from Joe, wanted one. She knew they were looking pretty domestic already with their dating and spending so much time together with the kids, and without them.

She reached out. *"Joe?"*

She watched him, noticing how smooth it was for him. She wondered if anybody could know when they were talking telepathically since he didn't give it away with his expressions or his actions. *"What do you think about a kiss hello?"*

"I think that's the closest I'm going to get to what I want to do with you right now."

She walked to him then, just those three little steps, and enjoyed the friendly kiss they could share in front of the teens.

Joe kept his hands to himself both because he didn't want to get her dirty and because he knew he was an example to the guys of how you act in front of other people with a lady.

"Are you staying for dinner?" Dana stayed close after the kiss. That connection, that soft heat, was addictive.

"If you're offering, we'll stay, as long as you let us wash the dishes afterward." He knew it was taking some getting used to for her. Apparently her husband had mistaken her for a maid during their marriage.

"How do you feel about veggie tacos, rice, and beans?"

"I think if you make it, it'll at least be good. Honest truth? If someone else said that to me I might have been really busy right about now."

"Your vote of confidence moves me. Thanks for that. *Sexy.*" She added that last part for just the two of them.

"You wrote the book on sexy, babe. And, uh, for the record, I'd like to get you alone for a few hours."

"What're you doing Thursday? While they're at school?"

"The usual. I'll move things around."

"Umm, good."

"Guys, let's wash up and help Dana with those groceries. If I know her there's a bunch more in the car."

Over veggie tacos filled with potatoes and soy meat, everyone shared their day. When the din had settled down, Dana broke in with some news.

"Hey, guys, as you know we've got a change in schedule coming up here. My new book releases soon so we'll be doing a tour in two weeks." She reviewed for Carter and Joe's benefit. She continued for all of them, "The surprise is that grandma and grandpa Robin are meeting us in New York to take you sightseeing while I work. Do you need anything for the trip you haven't mentioned? We'll be gone for a week and a half."

"Cool. TV?" Jason was relaxing now, getting ready to dig into homework.

"Some TV, radio, signings, the usual."

"I like when those come around on our breaks. Going with her is fun." Jenny put a hand to her stomach, happy and full.

Carter gaped. "You're going to be on TV?"

"I have the Ophrah show, Food Network, and a morning show. Four book signings and two radio interviews."

His mouth hadn't closed. "You know Ophrah?"

"I met her last year. It's a nice show."

This was the part that baffled Joe when he bothered to think about it. Without The Dreaming Joe could believe that he had simply stumbled into a perfect relationship for him and for Carter with a gorgeous, sweet, and hugely successful woman. With The Dreaming he knew now that no one had chanced into anything. It was meant. For all of them.

The Dreaming

He felt they were handling things well. Dana's absence from The Dreaming frustrated him a little bit. He wanted to show her more about it but she just hadn't been there since the dream she had with all the 4's. Heck, he just wanted to see her there. Be with her when she slept. Their schedules, their success in life, their dedication to the kids they were raising, had kept them in their own beds at night. So far.

"What's the new book?" asked Joe.

"'Dana Cooks Healthy Food for Kids.' When I get back I'll start in on the discovery phase of 'Dana Bakes for the Holidays.' I apologize in advance for baked goods overload. There's a minimal amount of bad stuff in there since I'm all about the healthy food, but it's still going to be a lot of giftable stuff, family projects, that type of thing. The testing will be different, too. We'll be baking together on some of the nights so I can see how it works for everyone."

"That's different, mom. Whose idea was that?" This came from Jason.

"Mine. We always do it so I thought it made sense to put it in a book with the normal pictures, how-to's, and stories. A lot of times it's presented as a craft idea in craft books, or books specific to baking with kids. My idea is to do a little here and there. Some traditional recipes like sugar cookies, gingerbread men, pie, and then some fancier stuff for people who get into it. We'll probably have a photographer at some point to come in and take pictures of us actually doing it to see if they work into the book."

"Finally!" Jenny was excited about being seen in one of her mom's books.

Dana could only sit back and laugh.

"Do you, get, like, recognized?" Carter wanted to know.

"By my fans, sometimes. It's not over the top like it would be if I was an actress first or something like that. I don't think I'd want that kind of fame."

"We'll be photographed, hmm?" Joe was considering what Beth might think of that. Carter's mother might be drawn to the glitter of what she thought Carter was into now.

"If you like. If they use the pictures we can leave your names out of it." She read his concern, but didn't understand it.

Seeing that, Joe clued her in. *"Carter's mom likes money. She might think he's getting something out of it. Something that could get her something. Let's just leave our names out of it. I like the idea of being a part of this book from the beginning."*

"The first part of testing is way different from what you guys have been eating. She'll have like 10 different sugar cookies and we'll have to talk about them all after we taste them, then we'll see like 20 different pieces of pie." Jason was complaining cheerfully.

The Dreaming

"You say that like it's a bad thing." Dana was famous for that smirky look in her face and voice.

"You have to admit it's more fun for you than it is for us."

"Hmm, if you want I'll find someone else to feed those mini pecan tarts to."

"Mini pecan tarts?" Jason sat up straight in his chair and they all shared a laugh.

Chapter 12

"Hey."

"Hey." She heard Joe's soft chuckle. *"I'll be there in about 10."*

She tried to contain her excitement. Her lust. She had an appalling image of ripping his clothes off and doing whatever she wanted to him. Regardless of what he wanted.

"Dana?"

"Right, 10. I'm...ready." Drowning. On fire.

She chose lingerie. She knew it would have been no less sexy if he found her in jeans and a tank top. It was just more layers to get through to what she wanted. What they both wanted. What they had waited more than long enough to have together.

Joe walked to the front door, thinking of the first time it opened to him, not knowing that he was meeting THE ONE. Had she looked at him and only seen another dad?

He pressed the button and listened to the happy

bells bounce around inside the house.

"Come on in, Joe, and lock the door behind you." She paused. "Please."

He followed her voice, rounded the corner to her bedroom, which he had only seen in passing. There were flowers on the borders, dusty roses, a charming white iron framed bed, and....

He swallowed.

Dana stood in front of him in a sheer black peignoir that tied at her breasts. There was something barely covering the vee at her thighs, also black.

They stood there for moments. Neither moved. Neither spoke.

Dana made the move, pressing a button on the stereo to play her favorite Savage Garden song, "Truly, Madly, Deeply." She walked to him then, moved into his arms, felt him pull her in and press her close.

She opened the buttons her head pressed against, kissed the warm skin beneath them. "You're overdressed, Joe."

"I don't think you'll let me stay that way for long."

She answered by flicking the clasp open on his belt. "Did I misunderstand why you wanted hours alone with me?" She husked the words into his ear, kissing the curve of it. Suckling. Enjoying the pulse that jumped in his neck under her lips.

"Dana." He breathed her name.

"Joe." She released the button of his jeans, her eyes on his. Her new feline smile curved her glossy lips.

"So you want it like that? You want me to throw you on the bed and go for it?" He thought he had pictured it enough to know how he wanted her. He was actually worlds away from having any idea.

"I feel like I've waited forever for this. I want to be with you, Joe."

"Kiss me, Dana."

He lowered his head to hers, parting her lips, diving in, and leaving her breathless.

Their lips moved over each other, their hands soft and fluttery, exploring places they had kept for this moment.

They moved to the bed, almost as if they were dancing there on purpose. Smooth.

She laid down on the bed, Joe covering her body completely. His clothes disappeared. Her seduction had somehow vanished. His lips stayed with hers while his hands were busy massaging her folds, stroking her clit. His eyes stayed on hers, shining with how much he was enjoying himself. And her.

She was molten. Languid. Boneless.

She followed the movement of his hand down between his thighs. There was so much she longed to do to him. With him.

She saw him slide the condom over himself, and

reached down to help him smooth it in place. She stroked the length of him, secretly cheering that there was so much of him.

"Nice try, but there are no secrets here, Dana. And thanks."

His lips found hers again, his hands cupped her ass, lifted her hips to slide deep inside of her.

"Oh, Joe," she moaned into his mouth. Her hands urged his long even strokes to come faster. She wrapped her legs around his waist, pressed her breasts against his chest, arching to him.

"Dana, oh, god." The feel of her around him, the blending of them to where they were only one person, totally immersed in the other, sent pleasure through him he had never even guessed at.

She gripped him in her inner muscles, squeezed him with blinding pleasure, massaged him with them, to where he had no choice but to urgently rush to his climax.

That feeling, the feeling of him lengthening inside her, harder than she had ever felt, pushed her over. Her walls pulsed around him. Her moans fevered his brain, his hands, his breath.

He groaned loudly. So loud Dana knew that if anyone had been in the house at that moment they would have heard it from one end to the other.

She reveled in the feel of him pulsing inside her, coming inside her.

They gripped each other as their heart rates slowed, their blood cooled.

"So, uh, Dana, I think it's official now."

The words held no meaning. She enjoyed hearing them from her ear pressed to his neck, feeling his throat move as he spoke them. Loved feeling his heavy weight pushing her down into the bed.

"Dana?"

"Hmmm?"

He had no choice but to laugh at that. "I said you're mine now."

"Yours?" Sleepy, dreamy, replete.

"Are you okay, babe?"

"You were already mine, Joe. I was already yours."

"Ain't that the truth...Dana, I love you." He stroked her hair tenderly, kissed her softly.

"I love you, too, and it's nothing like I thought love was. I love romance novels, and they make it really appealing, really...dream like. But this, this is so much more than that. I didn't know it could be like this."

"You're so much more woman than I ever knew there could be. And I've met some cool women in my time."

She smothered his laughter with her pillow.

Chapter 13

Joe and Dana waded side by side into the crystal blue pond. She was startled to see him sink lower and lower into the water, while the water stayed waist level for her. Maybe the pond was deeper where he was walking? Even if it was right next to her?

Joe continued to sink into the water with no attempt to stop it. When the top of his head was submerged she walked a few steps forward, then waited for him to reappear.

When he didn't reappear she decided to go under to look for him. In front of her she could see Joe walking along, several feet under the still surface of the pond.

You appeared beside her, floating on his hover board.

"Oh, I get it now." Looking around her with new eyes she couldn't believe that it hadn't occurred to her that she was in The Dreaming.

Up ahead Joe was waiting for her to cross the doorway into a huge, fabulously beautiful...sand castle?

"It's something, isn't it?"

"So you've been here before?"

"Yeah. This is where Riddle lives. This isn't a place that I can come to on my own, I can only come here when he summons me. Whatever he says, Dana, take it seriously. If the riddle is for you, write it down when you wake up. He doesn't mess around."

She reached for Joe's hand, tangling their fingers as they walked along the sandy floor. Brightly colored fish and mermaids swam around them. There were fascinating scenes etched into the sandy walls of pyramids, goddesses, the moon, flowers, bible stories, and people, from what she could see. The detail was exquisite.

One of the mermaids, a gorgeous, busty blond with hair to her waist (and no shells) swam to them. Her scales shimmered lilac when she moved. "Joe, you've been away for so long."

Joe lifted their locked hands to wave to her. "Hi, Velvet, this is Dana. Dana, this is Velvet."

She had seen Joe mildly nervous before, but this had to be the most nervous she had ever seen him.

Velvet stopped where she was and giggled. "I know that was done with a long time ago." And to

The Dreaming

Dana, "He's precious, isn't he? So sweet. I love when he comes to see Riddle."

"*A mermaid?*" She thought to Joe. "*Really?*"

She looked at him when he didn't answer. He was definitely embarrassed, his cheeks pink with it.

His grin was crooked and a little strained.

"It's nice to meet you, Velvet. Is this your home?"

The buoyancy of the water moved Velvet's hair around her, exposing her nipples and perfectly sculpted breasts.

Somehow, there was water everywhere, but nothing was actually saturated enough with water to be wet.

"I guess you could say that. I stay here most of the time."

I'm talking to a mermaid, one that Joe knows well enough to be embarrassed about. Can you believe this?

Joe led them into a room, the doorway arching wide at the top. There were words and numbers floating everywhere in the room.

"*Is it okay to touch the words, Joe? I want to see what they feel like.*" She wondered if they felt as soft as the "water" they walked in.

"There's Riddle. I'll introduce you. He won't answer questions or converse with you. He'll have one message and that'll be that. We'll be back up at the surface right after he tells us what we need to know."

Riddle was a good name for what she saw in front of her. His head was where others usually had their knees, resting on his feet, which rested on the sandy floor. His arms came out of his head, where his ears should be, his chest rested on top of his head, and his legs were on top of his chest. His ears were located on his knees. His groin was bare and sexless.

Riddle shifted so that (he?) looked right at her. Joe had said "he" right?

Meant to relax
But far from the mark
Chance the shun
The task is done

The words floated into place as he spoke them, zooming through the doorway from the hall, the word "shun" came off the wall it had been etched on. In the end the words lined up, some of them shiny, some of them packed sand, others looked like they had been typed in black or colored ink.

"Thank you for that, Riddle." Dana tried for gratitude in her tone. Her usual composure was inundated by the fantastic sight of Riddle.

To Joe's surprise Riddle spoke to Dana. "I've

The Dreaming

waited a long time to meet you, Dana. You're everything I pictured. Please do come back some time. Here is a special gift for you." Riddle's face broke into a wide smile as his arms extended to Dana. He placed a drop of oil in her palm.

Dana woke in the morning to the familiar sounds of her home on a Saturday morning and absolute silence from the kids' rooms. She was the first to wake.

She stretched, yawned, covering her mouth with her hand. She laughed at herself for that. There was no one watching her yawn.

What's that smell? Dana wondered, sniffing at her hand. Hmm. It was familiar but she couldn't place it.

The dream came back to her slowly and she realized then that Riddle had rubbed this oil into her palm. She shook with the knowledge, alarmed for the first time since she had learned about The Dreaming. Was everybody there trustworthy? What if she woke up with something besides scented oil in the palm of her hand, like poison? What if Joe was crazy and...

She had to stop right there. Joe was anything but crazy and if The Dreaming was dangerous he would have said something to her about it. His one warning was not to think of it as not affecting what he called "The World." He was right on with that.

The riddle came back to her then. She went to her office and wrote the riddle down on a lined pad, word for word. She hoped.

Chapter 14

Her first glimpse of Joe's ranch had been in The Dreaming, and it hadn't done justice to the actual beauty of his home and the land surrounding it.

There was lots of sand, naturally, since they lived in the land o' sand. She recognized huge Mormon teas, old leaning Joshua trees, beaver tail, and barrel cactus dotted across the sand.

She guided the minivan over the long driveway, curiously taking in the big fenced areas, the buildings, and the beautiful horses standing and playing in what she thought was called a paddock. A mother and her baby raced together at one end, while others stood calmly staring at nothing. They ranged in color from white, to gray, to a deep black.

Joe, Carter, and a woman she didn't know were standing near the rail of the biggest paddock, watching the horses and talking.

Dana paused the Honda where Joe pointed and

watched his long legged stride coming to meet them. Carter stayed at the fence with the woman.

"Welcome to Sunny Skies Stables." He was proud of what he had here. He was, finally, home.

"It's huge. And beautiful. I have a thousand questions!" Dana bubbled at him while she, Jenny, Jim, and Jason got out of the minivan.

"Hey, Joe." Jason knew his way around, having spent time there with Carter the last couple of months. He walked to meet him at the fence, bobbing his head and putting his hands in his pockets as he was introduced to the visiting woman.

Joe reached for Dana's hand, leaning in for a kiss hello and greeting Jenny with a hug in his other arm. He wore a hat, as he usually did on the ranch. Jeans that fit like a second skin showed off his strong thigh muscles and excellent ass, giving Dana a little shiver. Boots and a short sleeved shirt rounded out his everyday outfit. He nodded to Jim. "I'm Joe."

"Hey." Jim leaned against the silvery blue door, wanting to look like he was comfortable with where they were, and what they were doing.

"Nice hat," Dana murmured against his lips while she enjoyed the feel of him so close to her. It was her first experience of Joe, the successful rancher. *"You have to know you look irresistible in that hat. Is that why you don't wear it in front of me?"*

The Dreaming

"It's one of my favorites. How does it look on you?" He pinched the rim of the black hat with silver trim between his fingers and plopped it onto her head.

"Let's see." She considered in the mirror, happy to see that he liked the look of her in his hat by the way he smiled when he watched her, like a cat getting ready to eat the canary. "It looks alright."

She nodded and dropped the hat back onto his head.

"How about it, Jenny? Want to try it on?" Joe offered the hat to her with an easy, comfortable smile. "I hope you ladies will consider wearing hats on a regular basis, it makes the world a more beautiful place. Me, I just wear them to keep the sun out of my eyes."

"Joe." Dana breathed the dreamy word at him.
"Hmmm?" He drawled back to her.

She flashed an image to him of the two of them making love in what she thought his bedroom might look like, showing them rustling over the sheets, their bodies shining wet with the heat they made.

He smiled, masking his erotic thoughts from everyone else. *"You are just full of good ideas, babe...I'm getting you a hat, you know, for my part of the fantasy."*

"Come on over here and meet Cathy. She's here with her mare, Delilah, for breeding with Medallion.

We're going to get them acquainted in a few minutes. I had hoped they would arrive tomorrow but Delilah seems to be ready today."

"Which one's Medallion?" Jenny looked over the horses as they approached the fenced area.

"He's in the small paddock with the teasing fence. I usually keep him separated since he's mostly for studding."

"What's a teasing fence?" Jenny asked.

"It's a way to see if the mare is interested in being covered without putting them in together. This time of year I'm not looking to have too many mares in foal, that was a couple of months ago. I may bring a few mares out to see who's interested in Medallion today and see about adding maybe just one or two more babies to the program."

"Cathy, this is my lady, Dana, her daughter Jenny, and Jenny's boyfriend, Jim. You just met her son Jason here," he pointed to Jason. "Jason's been here a few times and the others are getting their first look at the ranch today."

"Nice to meet you all." Cathy had a soft voice, a soft look about her. She was about the same age as she and Joe, Dana estimated. And maybe just a tad unhappy that Joe wasn't single. She caught the longing look she cast Joe's way as he entered the arena and lead a horse away from the others and into the smaller area where the huge black horse watched

The Dreaming

him with interest.

"Same here," Dana answered. "So is that Delilah he's leading out?"

"Yes, that's my baby. Joe and I bred her mother to get her. He delivered her and trained her for me. This is her first attempt at foaling. I was very excited when Joe told me he had purchased Medallion along with Sunny Skies Stables. Isn't he magnificent?"

Dana wondered if the wistful look was for Medallion or for Joe. "He's gorgeous." The answer was the same either way.

"Carter, can you get Sunshine for me? We'll see what she thinks of Medallion today." He turned to Jason, considering. "Jason, you want to see about bringing Moonlight out for us? She's got a lead rope on." Jason might just have a way with the horses. If that was true, he was in the right place. Time and opportunity were there for all of them.

Sunshine was aptly named for the sparkle in her dark eyes and the yellow tint to her hair. Moonlight was white, shiny, and sleek. They seemed utterly at peace.

Jason followed him in. "Thanks, Joe."

They led the three horses in a line into the smaller arena, Joe staying with the teens, explaining that this was the end of the ranch's breeding program for the year.

Joe's love for the business was rooted in breeding and training sound, good natured pleasure horses that would be great companions for their owners throughout their lives together.

Dana watched a whole new phase of their world open before her. She was falling in love with the view, the land, and the animals. The feeling swamped her, her breath catching in her throat at the reality of the man she loved and the life he lived. The life they were sharing.

The mares were in the small arena now, on the opposite side of the teasing fence from Medallion. He stood near his side of the teasing fence, scenting the mares.

"Can we go closer?" Jenny called to Joe.

"Sure, come on over here. We're just watching what they do now."

One of the stately mares, Sunshine, lifted her tail, the action seeming significant to Dana's untrained eye. "I'm guessing that Sunshine is showing the most 'interest'?"

"Yep, so far. It looks like she'll get her twenty minutes with Medallion today and a couple more times before her estrous is over." The need to touch her was overwhelming. He went to her then, pulled her into his side, and hooked a finger through her denim belt loop.

The teens stood together, talking about the end of

The Dreaming

the school year that was only days away now.

Jenny glanced over to where her mother stood leaning into Joe. "Aren't they cute?" She sighed to no one in particular.

"Yeah, it's alright, them being together." Jason agreed with his twin. He didn't completely get how mooney-eyed it made Jenny, but he liked seeing his mom with that happy smile that he was beginning to think was permanent.

Carter and Jim were more interested in talking about their summer vacation plans. Jim was going to France with his French class and talking about how different it was for teens there than here in the U.S.

"You know what's weird? They never talk on the phone." Jenny's brow creased as she realized how strange that was to her. She thought back over the last couple of months, how her mom talked to Lucy, her grandparents, her editor, her agent, other people, but not Joe. She shrugged it off. Maybe she would be like that when she was older, and not need to talk to Jim every night even after they spent the day together at school.

"Twenty minutes? Why twenty minutes?" Dana watched Delilah and Moonlight, who didn't seem to be at all interested in Medallion.

"That's about all they need." He turned to Cathy. "Cathy, do you want me to bring The Duke in and see if he gets a better reaction? Delilah looks ready to me, but maybe The Duke can stir her up a little more, then we'll bring Medallion back."

She nodded her agreement.

"I'll be right back. You want to come with me, babe? Meet Medallion close up?"

She considered. He looked friendly enough, even if he was huge. "Yeah, I think I do."

He led her into the arena, fingers wound around each other.

Medallion watched her, intelligence and some kind of pride in his eyes.

"Medallion knows he's top stallion around here. He's gentle in spite of it, as long as you're not another stallion."

They led him back to the big barn where Joe put him in a roomy stall that smelled fresh despite what she thought it might smell like inside. "I'll get The Duke now. He's chestnut, not a black like Medallion. Somehow the mares go for him a little more, but Medallion gets the job done more often, if you get my meaning."

"Did this seem a little odd to you when you first started learning about it? You know, if I was trying to get pregnant, I don't think Ben would have sent me out to dinner with you to get me in the mood."

"No offense to the departed, babe, but I doubt Ben would have let you anywhere near me if that was the case. I know I wouldn't have. No, we play

The Dreaming

it a little different with breeding than that. We want to increase our chances of getting these mares in foal. In some cases people are driving across the country to get to the stallion they want."

She knew then that Ben's indifference would have surprised Joe, and that Joe would likely never be indifferent to another man showing interest in her.

"You know something, Joe? Your friend Cathy has a crush on you. She was just a little disappointed to meet me today." They were, blissfully, alone. "And you know what?" She flirted with her body and her eyes, brushing her breast against his arm as she spoke in a sultry voice. "I have one on you, too."

His answer was to pull her close and take the kiss he never stopped craving, the deep sweep and laving of tongue against tongue. His hands cupped her face, his body pressed her back to the wall.

They were brought back to the here and now by the loud throat clearing and bawdy smile of Joe's foreman, Stan. "Hey, Joe. Miss."

"Stan, this is Dana, Jason's mom. Dana, this is my foreman, Stan."

"Hi," she reached a hand out to shake his.

Joe couldn't blame Stan for the appreciative look in his eyes as he kissed Dana's hand in his own, more personal greeting. He drew the boundaries right there. "I imagine you'll be seeing my lady around here from time to time." The tone was one all men recognized. It clearly said *mine.*

"It'll be my pleasure." Stan saw the reaction his words and action brought out in Joe. So the boss had it bad for her, did he? He supposed if he saw her first he'd be in the same position.

"We're taking The Duke out to the teasing fence. Delilah and Moonlight don't seem too interested in Medallion just yet. Sunshine's ready for him. We'll be leaving once Cathy's ready to go. You can handle the rest until I get back tonight, right?"

"Yeah, I've got it all under control. You go enjoy yourselves." He'd be off once Joe got back and he'd be back again in the morning to supervise caring for the horses in the cool morning hours before the thermometer registered blistering triple digits. The worst of the heat would show itself in a couple of months when the humidity kicked in.

Chapter 15

Deciding where to eat the celebratory dinner with six different personalities was entertaining. To start off with, Dana wasn't a dictator type when it came to things like that. Yes, it was "her" night, but even on Mother's Day and her birthday she didn't run over the opinions of her family and friends. Much. She did draw the line at Jason's passionate plea for McDonald's. She understood that he was really after the novelty of seeing his mother eat a Big Mac and fries, but he was just asking too much. If she had agreed on the golden arches she would have eaten a salad.

They had enough time to enjoy their dinner at a leisurely pace before the movie started.

Jim and Jenny had been a couple for about three months, Dana remembered, watching them. He had thrown an arm around Jenny at the booth and then dropped it again when he was met with Joe's interested stare.

Dana felt especially warm then, right where her heart was already beaming over from Joe being so thoughtful to take all of them out to celebrate the publication of her new book.

They had settled on a very good Thai restaurant just blocks from the Carapelli's house. It was one of their town treasures, in Dana's opinion. She enjoyed every meal she'd ever had there.

The movie was equally fun to come to an agreement on. What Dana wanted to see was too girly for most of the group. Jenny might have gone along with her if she felt strongly about it. Dana played the "her" night card there by making sure she didn't have to see the latest comedic parody movie where, even she admitted, she would laugh at least once. The rest of the time she would be groaning and covering her eyes. Joe was neutral on all of the choices, his only goal centered on making sure that she enjoyed her evening. It was clear to him that she couldn't do that if the group didn't.

One of the major draws to the restaurant was the family-style dining. It gave everyone a chance to try things they weren't sure enough about to order.

The Thai iced tea was a huge hit with everyone. The orange tinted Mee krob slightly less so. It was one of Dana's favorites and what she thought of when she thought of eating there.

The Dreaming

"So Lavender's having this big party in a few weeks. She has friends that fire dance and she's invited us."

Dana focused in on Jenny's passionate declaration. It was the first she had heard of this party. She knew some things about Lavender, Jenny's coworker at It's You, but as far as she knew they usually didn't talk outside of the store.

"Will her parents be there?" Dana wanted to know.

"Mom, she's 19. She doesn't live with her parents anymore." Jenny delivered the news in a tone that said, "And isn't she lucky!"

She wanted to bristle but the memories of wanting to be out from under her parent's thumbs when she was Jenny's age were still too fresh. Jenny had a lot more freedom than she had at the same age, but she still had limits that her daughter considered old fashioned.

"Who else will be there?" Dana tried the buddy approach to getting the information she needed to decide whether this was one of those things she would dig her heels in on or not. She trusted Jenny's level head or she wouldn't have let her buy a car and work at her age, but she still wanted to know more about the blossoming friendship with Lavender-no-parents-at-home.

"Everyone! I HAVE to go, mom."

"Are you going?" Dana asked Jason.

"I'm working that day." He was more interested in his pad Thai than the conversation.

"Jim?" Dana turned to the boyfriend she was still getting to know. She knew his mother in passing from living in the same town for years, but they didn't have a friendship. He really hadn't spent any time at the house in the months that he and Jenny had been dating, which was one of the reasons why she invited him along tonight.

"Jenny and I are planning on it," he answered casually. "It sounds like it could be fun. Lavender's nice."

"Mom, I've known Lavender for like the whole six months she's been working at the store. She's totally *responsible*. Everyone likes her." Jenny pulled out the word she knew her mother was so fond of.

"Okay then and you know what to do if you see anyone drinking or using. Get home. Immediately." There was no way Dana's parents would have let her go to a party like that when she was Jenny's age. So far they hadn't run into any major problems with what Dana's parents thought of as her "liberal" parenting.

Joe watched the exchange with interest. He was considering letting Carter buy a truck with the money he was saving. His biggest concern was the

The Dreaming

freedom it would give Carter to roam without having to tell him where he was because he wouldn't need his dad's truck, or even his knowledge of where he was, to get him there and back.

"*Does it scare you, Dana? Jenny's got a boyfriend and a car. That can add up to some kinds of trouble.*"

"*It does scare me a little, Joe, but I wouldn't have let her have the car if I thought she was going to make really bad decisions. I'm still getting to know Jim. He's the unknown for me. What do you think about him?*"

"*That's sort of delicate, Dana. I keep thinking about what was on my mind when I was their age and sometimes opportunity was the only thing that kept me out of a girls pants.*"

"*I don't think they're there yet, but I'm watching. Believe me when I say that I'm watching.*"

"*Mind if I watch along with you? You're doing an excellent job with your kids, but I think two heads are better than one, in our case. I'm totally comfortable where you're concerned with Carter.*"

"*I saw the look you gave Jim earlier, so I guess you're already doing that,*" she teased.

"*Sorry if I overstepped. This is pretty new for me.*"

"*Let's just see how it goes, it's worked for us so far. The look was fine with me.*" She put a hand on his arm. *"I appreciate your vote of confidence with Carter. You're doing great with him."*

Carter cleared his throat a few times before they heard him. They were still eating, but neither of them were talking, and Carter had asked his question three times. Man, they were wrapped up in each other.

"Sorry, what was that?" Joe flushed a little. At least he hadn't been fantasizing that time.

"I asked what you think about Delilah. When she left I felt like you had done a lot with her, but now she's looking even better."

"I think Cathy's doing very well with her. On that subject, do any of you, besides Carter and Jason, know how to ride?"

"I went on a couple of trail rides." Jim swallowed and met Joe's eyes for the first time. "My mom likes to do that on vacations."

"Did you like it?" Carter asked. Shyly. Jim was pretty popular at school and he felt like if he said the wrong thing it might get around. Not that many of the kids at school lived on working ranches like his. Anything that made you stand out was something someone could use against you.

"It was okay, I guess. Last time I got this horse called Pepper. At first I didn't know why they called it that because it seemed like it barely moved. Then it kept biting the tail of the horse in front of it and

The Dreaming

stopping to eat the sand."

"That sounds like a trail horse that could use my dad's training."

"How do you teach a horse to stop biting another horse?" Jason asked, totally comfortable.

"Carter?" He gave his son a chance to talk about something he was good at.

"It depends on the horse, but I think that it's good to compliment them most of the time. Treats are good, too, but sometimes they get to where they'll only do what you want if they get the reward and that can lead to problems." He saw his dad nodding in approval.

"When I was in junior high, that's what we called middle school back then, I had a friend who's sister had horses about a half an hour away from where we went to school. We were allowed to ride if we mucked out the stalls. The horses were in them when we worked and that was pretty scary for me. I was always afraid of getting kicked. They were just teaching me how to clean out the horses' hooves when we stopped going there," was Dana's answer to Joe's query.

"You've ridden your friend's horse a couple of times since then, right, mom? Stacey?" Jason snitched a fried shrimp that was hidden under the pile of sweet, crispy Mee krob noodles.

Dana nodded her head to answer Jason.

"Hey!" Jenny protested.

Dana smothered a laugh. They had ordered extra shrimp with the appetizer for that exact reason, and portioned them out when the appetizer came to the table.

"What?" Jason asked around the fried shrimp he was already chewing.

"All right, all right. I propose a toast, with this tea," Joe grimaced, "to Dana. Congratulations on the release of your new book and your publicity tour!"

The group raised their cups, some knocking them together just hard enough for Dana to check that they weren't cracked at the end of the toast.

Jason shouted, "Awesome, mom!" Jenny sang a melodious "Woo hoo," making Dana smile. Carter gave a passionate "Right on!" Jim was silent.

Jason continued the toast, "To traveling to New York, L.A., Philadelphia, and Houston!" The group clinked and drank again.

"You're empty, dad." Carter laughingly tried to pour more tea for Joe.

"Shh, no one was supposed to know," he scowled at his son.

"To hanging out with grandpa and grandma Robin!" Jenny raised her cup, the others riding the excitement.

"To Jim's trip to France. You'll have to tell us all about it when you get back." Dana included him by toasting to his exciting summer plans.

She saw Carter's withdrawal then. He didn't have any exciting summer plans to toast to. Joe saw it, too.

"To Carter's first truck!" Joe raised his empty cup.

"Good one, Joe."

"I figure you'll be around to help me navigate the sand traps."

"I figure that, too. He'll be fine," she soothed.

Carter grabbed Joe for a hug. "Thanks, dad." He hid a sniffle.

Chapter 16

Meredith and George Robin welcomed their family with wide smiles and open arms in the hotel lobby.

"You've grown a foot since the holidays, Jason!" Grandma Robin measured him with her eyes, holding back tears at how fast her grandchildren were growing.

"Come here, sweet pea, let me look at you," George held his arms wide for Dana. "You look gorgeous. We may have to start cooking like you if it makes you glow like that."

"Hi, dad," she said around his enthusiastic hug.

"It isn't her food that's making her happy, it's her new boyfriend," Jenny ratted her out in the first sentence.

"What's this? Where is he? Afraid to meet the parents?" He went into protective dad mode. He figured he'd missed the mark with Ben. The man had been decent enough, but he hadn't given his daughter the happiness he'd always wanted for her.

The Dreaming

She laughed. "No, dad, I don't think he's afraid to meet you. He's just working." Dads, she shook her head.

"How about it, Jase, is this guy good enough for your mom?" He purposely mirrored his grandson's cool guy stance.

"He's cool, grandpa. I knew him before she did."

"He treating you any different now that he's dating your mom?" George drew him away from the ladies and dropped his voice.

"He's around more, but that's about all. He helped me fix my car so I didn't have to take it to the mechanic, but he would have done that anyway."

"So you like him?" This was the first man the twins had mentioned their mother dating in specific. He was sure he hadn't heard the term boyfriend come out of either one of their mouths when they talked about the occasional date their mother went on.

"Yeah, I like him. I hang with his son Carter a lot. He's on the team with me and Jeremy."

"Your school did very well this year, Jason. Will you go out for the team again next year?"

"Yeah, we're good. I'm trying out for swim team next year, I think. Are our rooms all together?"

"Yep, we're on the same floor. This is pretty neat, isn't it, your mom hitting the big time with her cookbooks?"

"Sweet." His stomach growled, making the

reason for his short answer obvious.

"Do we have everything we need to go to dinner now?" Meredith gathered her family and sighed again at how happy she was that they were all together for almost two weeks.

"So this place is a big deal to you, right, Dana? You've always wanted to eat there?" George asked.

"I've been reading about this place for years. They're supposed to have some of the most cutting edge raw food in the country. You're not even going to know you're eating beets, dad. They'll make it taste like chocolate pudding or something equally delicious."

"This I have to see."

"Dana?"

"Hi, Joe."

"You sound relaxed. Are things going well?"

"They're going really well. How are things there?"

"If I don't think about not seeing you for a couple of weeks, I'm fine. Otherwise, I get lonely for you."

"Oh, Joe, that's so sweet. I miss you, too."

"But then again, we have a meeting in The Dreaming tonight, so it will be like we're together. Sort of."

"I love knowing ahead of time. I won't wear my

grungy pajamas."

"How 'bout you don't wear anything at all?" He asked in a sexy purr.

"Is that the kind of meeting we're going to have?" She got excited thinking about it. "It's already been too long since we made love."

"I want you day and night, Dana, and I don't know what kind of meeting we're having, just that we're having one."

"I'm already falling asleep. Are you tired?"

"Not quite, you're a little ahead of us there." He dropped his tone to the sexy low purr he knew she liked. "Take your clothes off, Dana. Writhe around on your bed and think of me."

"Is that what you're doing?"

"Babe, if we did it as much as I think about us doing it we'd never do anything else."

"Yes, we would Joe. We'd stop to eat. You need your strength for what I'm picturing."

He groaned clearly in her head, watching the erotic images she enjoyed so well. She was straddling him, cascading her silky hair through her hands, her generous breasts naked, his fingers stroking the nipples.

"God, babe, I'm on fire over here."

"Maybe I can help you with that fire." She pictured herself lowering onto his rock hard length, felt him filling and stretching her. She moved her

hips up and down, picturing his hands guiding her at her waist.

"You are very good at that. You're so beautiful, Dana." *He moaned when she changed the picture so that she was riding him harder, really feeling that he was actually inside of her.*

"Are you stroking yourself, Joe?" She purred to him.

"I don't have a choice, Dana. If I don't I'll explode."

"You do that, Joe. Explode for me."

"Are you close, Dana? I'm not going without you." He pictured himself with his head between her thighs, his tongue tasting her erotic flavor. He moved his tongue to inflame her. To make her come.

She caught his intense arousal then and felt it pulse through her core. She stroked her fingers over her clit, her breath coming harder as she got closer.

She heard and felt the same breathy panting coming from him, felt that her own response had pushed him over. His ecstatic moans pushed her over, her walls pulsed with her release.

"You really are the perfect woman, babe. You got us both off. I'm holding you now."

"I love being held by you. You're so cuddly." She snuggled into her pillow.

"You sound ready for sleep." He urged her to let go, too. He'd miss her, but he knew she was

working hard there and needed the rest. "Next time we talk we'll be in The Dreaming."

"It's a date."

"Good night, babe. I'll see you soon."

Dana stretched an arm out wide at her side, arcing it up and covering her yawn with her hand. The cool navy blue sheet slipped down, showing her naked breasts.

"Perfect," Joe nuzzled her nipple with his mouth, opened it, pulled it in. He moved his leg over, intending to hug her body beneath him. You floated beside the bed.

Dana moaned, eyes closed, her hands threaded with his soft brown hair.

"We have company, babe. It's You. We're in The Dreaming." Joe reluctantly covered them up.

"Whaaa?" She answered groggily.

"Hi, You. I trust you're doing well tonight?" Joe made conversation while Dana adjusted to the fact that they weren't alone and that they wouldn't be playing the fun game they were hoping for.

"I am well, Joe. You seem to be doing well also."

"Better than ever, You. But then, you'd know that, right?" His relationship with You was friendly and welcome. It was also very hard to define.

"I know that it will only get better." He floated, as expressionless as ever, unblinking. His robes didn't rustle when he moved. His hover board was completely silent.

"That's good to know. She's...amazing. Is she the one you told me about? Because if she isn't, I think I'm going to have to put a stop to whoever it was you said was coming for me and Carter. She's the one I want." He could hardly believe he was thinking that, let alone saying it aloud, and with her there to hear it.

"Do you truly want the answer to that question?" You responded.

That gave him pause. Did he? How would he deal with it if You said there was someone else for Dana? That's what it would boil down to, because she was perfect for him. If that was the case would it be better to know now, or live it and find out?

Either way, he knew he would live it and find out. The difference is that it would be easier, and also harder, to know the outcome while he was still living it.

But he wasn't in this alone. It was Dana's choice, too.

"Dana, are you...with us now?" He couldn't say awake, now, could he?

"Yeah. I'm hoping for a robe or something."

"I'll get that for you." He moved to the dresser in

his room and handed her a long t-shirt. He pulled on a pair of pajama bottoms for himself.

"I asked You a serious question, Dana. I asked him if you're the woman they told me about five years ago. You wants to know if I'm sure that I want to know the answer, but it's your answer, too. Do you want to know? Do you think either one of us should find out?"

She was covered up now and felt more comfortable with it. She had heard some of what Joe said, and knew more because she sensed his thoughts. Hurting him would never sit well with her, naturally. Maybe it was better if they did know what was ahead for them. They had been together for a fairly short time and if they were meant to end, if, all things good forbid, their happiness was temporary and Joe would find someone else in time...

"I want to know. It's better to know."

You turned to Joe, his hover board smoothly adjusting beneath him. "Are you sure that you want to know?"

He felt Dana's sadness at the possibility of losing something so precious when they had only just found it. Of hurting him.

He needed to know, too.

"Yes, You. We want to know."

You spread his arms wide and a huge book appeared in them. The book opened to a photograph of Dana and Lucy having lunch. The caption below it read "Dana is Falling in Love."

"Who is that?" Joe asked her.

"My best friend, Lucy. That's the day I told her about the dreams I've been having, and about you." She turned to You, knowing she was going to ask one of her limited questions. "I saw a flash out of the corner of my eye. Was that you taking this picture?"

"Yes."

"That's a simple answer to a complicated question," she grumbled, confused.

"That's new." Joe rubbed his jaw. "I don't think you've taken pictures of me in The World."

"That's new," You echoed.

"Is the answer to our question in this book?" Joe prompted.

"Yes."

The pages flipped on their own to a page with only one word written on it. While the pages flashed by, Dana caught glimpses of three different pictures of herself. In the first one she was sitting on a horse wearing a hat. In the second she was holding a baby. In the last she was standing next to Carter, who was laying in a hospital bed.

The single word printed on the page in front of them was YES.

Chapter 17

Dana sat in her place of honor, meeting the long line of fans she was autographing cookbooks for, and taking the occasional picture with a fan who brought a camera along.

George was glad that he had taken advantage of a quiet moment before it started to take a video of Dana, Jenny, and Jason sitting at the table together. The big cardboard cutout of Dana behind them made a perfect backdrop.

The next fan bubbled up to the table wearing a flowing yellow dress with huge brown fabric sunflowers all over it.

"Dana?"

"Hi, Joe." She smiled at the warmth she felt when she talked with him. *"I'm in a signing. Can't really talk now."*

"I'll catch you later, then. Dana? I wanted to say that I bought a copy of your book today. I had to order it on-line because the store sold out."

"Oh, Joe. Thats...wow. Thanks."

"Wow, you're telepathic!" The woman in front of her exclaimed. "And you're talking to," she paused then, concentrating, "your lover. I knew there was something I really liked about you!"

Dana was stunned, and had no idea what to say to her. Business, she reminded herself. Do what comes next. "How would you like me to sign this?"

Ivy tossed her waist length blond hair back over her shoulder. "For Ivy, that's I V Y, with love, Dana. Is that okay?" She looked at Dana, watching something just above her head, and then near her ears.

Dana felt an interesting warmth from the woman, like they were long time friends. Being a friendly person that wasn't entirely unusual for her, but there was something different about this feeling. It was clearer, somehow. And really strong.

"You're still getting used to it, aren't you?" Ivy felt the need to persist. She followed those urges every chance she got.

Dana met her eyes. "Yes, I am. You seem to know something about it."

"It took some time to get it working right, and I still can't do it with some of the people I really want to talk to, but I do know something about it." She was thrilled to be talking to Dana Carapelli about telepathy!

The Dreaming

Dana caught a scent as she opened the book to the front cover. It was familiar, but she couldn't place why. "What is that scent?"

"Oh, it's lavender oil. I think I splashed some on it. I was so nervous about meeting you. It's for calming you down, you know? It turns out I didn't need it after all. You're so nice!"

It struck her then, that it was the scent that was on her palm after the dream with the riddle. Wasn't lavender the name of the girl that had invited Jenny to the unsupervised party?

She'd have to look at it again but she thought the riddle had said something about "chancing the shun." She would be doing that, she supposed. Jenny wouldn't be happy with her when she told her she couldn't go, and to keep her distance from Lavender.

"Thanks, Ivy. I appreciate that. Could I get your number? I'm not sure why, but I feel like we should be able to get in touch."

I'm changing, Dana thought, and I'm not sure where it's taking me.

"Of course, it's..." Dana wrote the numbers as Ivy spoke them.

"Thanks so much. I hope you enjoy the book."

"Of course I will. I have all of your books." She patted her rounded belly. "I want to start my baby off right."

"Congratulations." She felt that overwhelming joy she always felt when she heard about or saw a new baby.

The store representative, Julie, stepped up then. "It's time for a very short break. Mrs. Carapelli will be back in five minutes."

Julie brought Dana to an office for the break, explaining, "She's obviously a nice person, but I thought that it might be hard for you to break away from her gracefully. Besides, you've been going for awhile now. Are you hungry, thirsty?"

"Not really. We ate very well before we got here, and I have water at the table. I appreciate you helping me with that. I think she's very nice, too."

"That's my job." Julie took the seat across from her. "We'll be back in just a few. Would you like a moment alone?" Truthfully, Julie just needed to be somewhere else in the store. There was just too much going on today.

"Sure, a moment to myself sounds good."

"I love this camcorder you guys sent us for Christmas. I didn't think I'd ever really use it, just wanted it to stay current with the technology. What they can do these days!" Grandpa enthused over the video he had taken of Dana and the twins.

"You know what we could do, grandpa? We could upload that video to youtube and Jim could

The Dreaming

watch it in France. Let's do it!" Jenny pushed to have her boyfriend see her on youtube.

"Yeah, I could upload it to my laptop and then we could post it on youtube." Jason thought it would be fun to show grandpa how to use his camcorder in a way that he maybe wouldn't figure out on his own.

"I could send it to Margie, too! That's just too amazing, what you can do in just a couple of hours if you have the right amount of money." Grandma shook her head, sharing in their excitement.

"Will great aunt Margie know how to watch the link, grandma?" Jenny relaxed with her family in the cafe portion of the bookstore.

"What does she have to do to watch it?"

"We'll e-mail the link to her. All she has to do is open the e-mail and click on the link. If her computer has a media player it will play automatically." Jenny checked her watch, noticing that they would only be in New York a couple more hours before they would be leaving to fly to Texas.

"What if she doesn't have that? She has an e-mail. I taught her how to open files with attachments a few years ago so she could see pictures of you guys."

Jason answered, "The computer will probably tell her what she needs to do to be able to see the video. The software is free. All she has to do is download it. Her computer is pretty sweet if she still has the one I saw there last year."

"It's the same one," grandpa confirmed.

"I think she'll be able to see it then. Want to do it now? I'll show you how to transfer the video onto the laptop and upload it to youtube."

"Have you ever posted a video before? I know you've posted comments and stuff like that." She thought her brother only watched youtube.

"I've seen Jeremy do it. You know how he makes those gameplay videos for Minecraft, Bioshock Infinite, and Halo 4?"

"Right." Jenny drifted away from the conversation then, satisfied that Jason did know how to post the video. She wasn't all that into video games.

Jason, grandma, and grandpa worked together on putting the video together while Jenny read Vogue.

Dana had been up for hours to meet the early taping time of the morning show segment where she made her version of macaroni and cheese. It was one of her personal favorites because if you didn't know it was healthy you would never guess that it was. She had tested it on everyone she could find that was a fan of the incredibly unhealthy original recipe that was known for its creamy cheese sauce. Now kids could enjoy a favorite meal without building a lifetime of destructive eating habits.

The Dreaming

She covered a yawn and was glad that there were only two more people in line for her. She was ready to be on the plane where she could sleep a little.

Chapter 18

"I feel like we haven't had two minutes alone this whole trip, Dana. I'm very curious about this new man I hear you're dating. I don't remember you saying anything about that to me. Am I forgetting or have you been keeping it to yourself?"

Meredith had Dana good and alone in the dressing room. This mall had the biggest Express they had ever seen and they hadn't been able to resist the huge SALE signs hanging from the ceilings and in the windows.

Dana sighed to herself. What was she supposed to tell her mother about Joe?

"At least tell me this," Meredith urged, "is the sex any good?"

Dana flushed.

Meredith was delighted. "Good! It's about time, Dana. I'm happy to see you looking so happy."

"You know what trips me up, mom? It's that I feel like I'm doing this for the first time, and I'm the

The Dreaming

mother of teenagers." Dana considered the clingy brown tank top in the mirror. And the way she looked in it. She was buying it.

Meredith sighed, about to admit something she hadn't planned to tell Dana. "I'm sorry that I never talked to you about men the way I should have. You were so quiet in high school it didn't seem to matter. Then you met Ben and things were going so well. You seemed to be perfect for each other." She sighed heavily now. "What Margie was going through with Cindy, running around wild with all of those boys and drinking, made me think you had it made. If I sensed that anything was lacking between you, I didn't say anything about it because I didn't want to take a chance that you would take up with someone really wrong."

She sat in the chair, considering her mother. She was an attractive, active, and vibrant 70 something. And she was far more guilty than Dana was comfortable with.

"It isn't your fault that my marriage was on the boring side, mom. He was basically good to me. It IS worlds away from what I'm experiencing with Joe."

Dana decided to open up to her mother about some of the thoughts she was going round and round with when she had time to think about it. Which she did since she hadn't seen Joe in a few days.

"This is what I'm worried about, mom. The first couple of years after Ben died I was only mildly curious about dating, and once I got a handle on it I didn't really meet anyone that mattered enough to have my days change over. I've barely been intimate with anyone since Ben, and he was my first. I don't know if you knew that." Did it ever get easy to talk to your mom about sex? She'd have to ask Lucy about it. If Lucy couldn't do it, then no one could.

"I suspected. Now I'm ashamed to admit that at the time I hoped that he was the only one. Now I wish I had encouraged you to date more before you got serious about Ben." Meredith replaced the tank on the hanger and handed Dana the formfitting soft brown jeans she had picked out for her.

"You know Jenny's had a boyfriend for about three months now, Jim? She's dated a couple of other boys, more than I did by her age. I'm always wondering what to say to her about him. My main concern is that she doesn't get too serious with him. They're so young."

"I think you're doing just fine with Jenny. She's mentioned Jim a couple hundred times. I don't think you have anything to worry about there."

The sales clerk smiled at the shared laughter she heard coming from the dressing room.

"Here's what I wonder about Joe, mom. I'm wondering if my life is going to become all about him, the way my life became all about Ben. I put everything on the back burner when I quit working before the twins were born. *My* life really started again after Ben died. I feel terrible just saying that."

Meredith gathered her daughter in a hug. "I couldn't be more proud of the way you live your life, Dana." She sniffled.

"Now, as for this Joe, is it that serious? Do you see yourself with him in the long run? You just said that you haven't dated all that much." She watched her daughter's face carefully. Saw it soften when she thought of Joe. Saw her put a fluttery hand to the pulse jumping in her throat and sigh a dreamy sigh.

"I see. Well, I've never seen you do that before." It made her smile. "Here's the thing, Dana. The trouble a good man brings to your life is more than worth it. You're much too intuitive to let someone close that won't appreciate you a second time."

"You think of me as intuitive, mom? I haven't really thought of myself that way."

That surprised Meredith. "Well, I suppose we've never talked about it, but yes, I think of you as intuitive. Your life runs very smoothly, Dana.

You seem to be in the right place at the right time and to do things that seem risky to me but seem to always work out for you."

Dana nodded, considering. That seemed reasonable to her.

"Your father wants to meet this Joe, you know."

Dana groaned. "Don't tell me he feels guilty about Ben, too."

"As a matter of fact, I think he does. He doesn't talk about it, you know, but a wife knows."

A bit of the imp that had passed through to Dana sparkled in her eyes. "So, do you have some really sexy under things to wear when you see Joe again?"

She groaned again, and covered her eyes.

"Come on now, Dana. Tell me you do or you don't. They have great things here. I was looking at that red nightie just outside the door. Did you see it?"

Dana had all new respect for her teens and their responses to her probing questions at the moment. "I have things, mom."

Meredith laughed then, earning the private nickname, Merry, her husband had given her.

"Should I get my own dressing room to try on the nightie? I don't want to embarrass your tender sensibilities."

"I don't think letting you try your lingerie on by yourself makes me overly tender. I think it makes me sane."

The light teasing carried through the wood between them when Dana passed the peignoir over the top of the door.

"Mom," Dana's tone was tender with emotion,

"thanks for talking to me about Joe. He's important, and you helped me see that he isn't the kind of man that would expect me to give myself up to suit him. I don't think he'd even let me do that."

"Then you should get one of these nighties. It's very flattering."

"Moooom," she thought she sounded just like Jenny.

"Jenny, there's something I want to talk to you about."

Jenny knew that tone. She wasn't about to get a raise in her allowance. "Yeah?"

"It's weird not having any privacy, isn't it? We've all been in each other's space since we started this trip." Dana was deciding whether or not to unpack. They would only be here for one night and she had bought two great outfits at Express.

"It's all pretty cool anyway. Jason's not that bad." She opened the bags from Express after she got the nod from her mom telling her it was okay for her to look in them. "Nice, mom."

"Jenny, it's about Lavender. I had a dream and there seemed to be a kind of warning in it. I think the warning is about Lavender."

Jenny rolled her eyes. "You just don't want me to go to her party because she's 19 and lives with roommates instead of her parents."

"No, I already said you could go to the party because I trust *you*. I think there's a real reason to stay away from Lavender." She gathered her courage for Jenny's reaction. "Not just from her party."

"I work with her, mom. What do you want me to do?" She didn't ask her mom if she was trying to make her look like a kid in Lavender's eyes. Her mom wasn't like that.

"I want you to keep your distance from her. You don't really spend time with her anyway, right?"

The paisley bedspread they laid on in Dana's attached room was truly insulting to the eye, but catching their breath after the ride from the airport was still the highlight of their busy day.

"I was just starting to. She brought me lunch a couple of times, and she asked me to a movie, but I was busy that night."

Dana stroked her daughter's arm. "Do you really like her?" She asked sympathetically. This seemed to be the day for mother-daughter heart-to-hearts.

Jenny cuddled into her mom's arms in a way she hadn't for a long time. They were both so busy. Quiet moments, just the two of them, were rare, with all the responsibilities at home.

"I think so. She's cool, you know? A lot of the kids I know her age don't pay any attention to me, but she does." Jenny's voice was muffled by sleep.

The Dreaming

"Can you do this for me, please? I know it seems a little strange, but I think it's really important."

"I'll do it, mom. I hope Jim understands. He was really looking forward to that party."

"If you want I'll tell him it's my idea. You don't have to take the rap."

She giggled. "Mom, it's waaay better coming from me. He's still, I don't know, getting used to all of us. He just lives with his mom, you know? There's so many of us."

She started to ask how the three of them could be counted as "so many of us," but Joe and Carter would seem like regulars at the house now.

"I trust you on that, Jenny. Thanks for making this easy for me."

"Mom," she asked tentatively, "do you miss Joe *all* the time?"

She *was* feeling like a teenager. "I miss him, Jenny. I miss Carter, too." That gave her an idea. "I'm gonna call him."

Jenny didn't hear her because she was asleep.

She dialed Joe's house from her cell.

Carter answered. "Hello?"

Dana's words filled with a smile. "It's Dana, Carter. I wanted to say hi. I was thinking about you and wondering how things are going."

He paused, surprised. When he saw her caller ID

he thought she was calling for his dad, but she didn't really call him, did she?

"Uh, things are okay. I miss eating at your house."

"Who is that, Carter?"

She heard Joe's voice in the background.

"It's Dana. She's calling to see how I am."

"I love you, Dana. Get your sweet ass home to me, would you?"

"My sweet ass will be home pretty soon."

"Well, go ahead and tell her then. Hey, Dana." He called out for Carter's benefit.

"Tell him I said 'hey' back."

"Don't you want to talk to him?"

"I'll talk with him later, Carter. Tell me about you."

Carter settled in, satisfied that she really did want to talk to him. "I'm working for my dad, earning my share of the money for my truck. He bought it for me. I just have to work the hours every week to make my payment to him. It's cool, Dana. Maybe I could take you out in it when you get back," he offered awkwardly.

"I'd like that, Carter. I'm glad it's working out for you."

She would like it, Carter realized. She liked him, too, not just his dad.

"Jason sent me the youtube link. Dad and I

watched it a little while ago. It looks like you had a big crowd in New York."

"Youtube? What youtube?"

"It's a video of you, Jason, and Jenny sitting at a table with stacks of books next to you and a big line of people in front of you. There's a big cut out of you behind the table."

"Right. I remember my dad taking that video at the first signing. What did you think of it?"

"It's okay," and not very important to him. "I hung out with Jeremy last week. We had him over for a riding lesson and steaks." His grin was huge. "It was Wednesday, we had to eat something special, you know?"

She was only a puddle of goo now, Dana thought. I don't just love Joe, I love Carter, too.

"Did you have vegetables with the steaks?"

He laughed. His dad's exact words when they shopped were, "We have to have vegetables tonight, Carter. She'll want to know that we're eating right."

"We had corn on the cob that a boarder grew and salad with the baked potato. It was pretty good."

"I'm glad to hear that, Carter. I'm gonna run now. We have a busy trip here and I need to catch some rest."

Chapter 19

Grandma, grandpa, Jason, and Jenny were eating lunch in the museum cafe at the J. Paul Getty in the San Fernando Valley as Dana taped a show in Burbank, CA.

The day was warm past the point of comfortable. The view of the valley was spectacular. The food was unbelievably good. They all knew that Dana would be glad that they liked it so much and sorry that she missed it.

They would all be going back to their daily routines in a couple of days. The grand finale was a trip to Universal Studios Hollywood for all of them.

Jason's ring tone sounded, a strange hip hop beat and lyrics that had both of his grandparents raising their eyebrows had him hiding a smile and wincing at the same time.

"Hello?" He didn't recognize the number.

"Hi, Jason. It's Sue." She leaned back against the pillows on her bed, giddy that she had his cell

The Dreaming

number.

Jason thought, Sue who?

She filled the silence. "I saw you on youtube. Everyone's talking about your big trip and your mom's book."

Could it be Sue Grady? But how did she get his number? It sounded like her. His heart started to thud.

Sue continued, "You must be having a great time traveling all over the place. The youtube said you were in New York for that."

"We were in New York. I posted the video." She sounded like they were friends, but they weren't, were they? Who was she?

"God!" She sighed. "Where are you now?"

"We're at a museum near L.A. We'll be back home in a couple of days." Risking sounding stupid he asked, "How did you get my number?"

"I asked around until someone gave it to me."

She sounded annoyed.

He tapped Jenny, pulling her aside to whisper, "Do you know anyone named Sue?"

"Yeah, Sue Templeton. Is that her? Why would she be calling you?" Jenny steered him closer to where their tour was meeting to look at sculptures. Grandma was in love with the museum and wanted to see all of it.

He shook his head no.

The voice on the phone kept talking, telling him how cool she thought it was that he was meeting all kinds of celebrities.

Jenny shrugged and leaned closer to the phone that Jason offered to listen.

"It's...Sue Grady? Why would she be calling you?" Jenny kept her voice low, hoping Sue wouldn't catch it. Sue was one person she didn't want paying any attention to her.

"Then we'll go to the mall. See you then." Sue ended the call.

Jason fanned himself with the menu he snagged for his mom from the fancy restaurant they had passed up in favor of the cafeteria style food they had eaten. His white shorts and blue tank top showed off his blue eyes and blond hair.

"I think she asked me out," he was clearly puzzled by it. He had fantasies about her. She was pretty in a sexy way, built, and popular. His fantasies seemed to be coming true.

"Really? Are you going to go?" Sue was far from Jenny's first choice of a girlfriend for Jason. She was mean with a capital M.

"What's all this?" Grandma saw those two heads together and it made her wonder. They got along well enough, but if they were planning something she'd better find out about it now. Together they were invincible.

The Dreaming

Jenny gave Jason the lead on answering, nodding his way.

"A girl I like just asked me out. I think."

The tour guide looked at them pointedly, giving Jason an escape from talking more about it with his grandma.

It was too important for Jenny to wait until later. She whispered as low as she could into his ear. "Jase, she's...not right for you."

"Stay out of it." He moved away, ending the conversation.

Outside once again they bought Italian sodas and sat near the fountains beneath the big shady trees.

"What was all that about in there?" grandma asked.

"You'd think we'd be used to all this heat, living in Arizona." Grandpa grumbled, sipping his too sweet lemon drink.

Jenny stayed silent. Jason didn't want *her* opinion of him going out with Sue.

"It's no big deal, grandma. I got a call and Jenny helped me figure out who was on the phone."

He tried to downplay it so they could all move on.

"Didn't you say that the girl asked you for a date?" There had to be something to it, Meredith thought. Jenny didn't say much of anything to or about Jason unless it mattered.

"Yeah, I think she did."

"You *think* she did? And you didn't know who she was?" She turned to Jenny. "Is she a friend of yours?"

Treading carefully Jenny answered, "No, I've never spent any time with her," because I avoid her like the plague. She finished the thought silently.

What was wrong here? Meredith bumped her husband, bringing his attention away from the sleek colored pigeons begging for bread. "Huh?"

"That case full of dishes was interesting, grandma. Do you like this museum better than the other ones we went to?" Jason went for a distraction.

"What did you find interesting about them?" She caged.

"They were all so different," he answered in a tone that said he wanted her to drop her real question.

She glanced at George. Seeing that he didn't want to spend the final days of their time with the grandkids arguing, she dropped it.

"I like this museum for antiquities, but nothing beats the Museum of Modern Art for," she laughed, "modern art."

"Joe?"

"Babe! How are you?"

The Dreaming

He was always so happy to talk to her. "I'm really good and ready to be home. How are you?"

"Things are going well. Delilah is in foal, Carter's working past what I'm asking for, and I had a nice offer for Sunshine. She'll go to a good owner that wants to ride and maybe breed her in the future."

"That does sound good. So Sunshine and Medallion didn't make it this time?"

"I have about a minute here, babe. I'm heading out to ride our trails and see if there's anything that needs to be fixed. They made it, but she didn't get pregnant."

"You work hard, Joe."

"Looks who talking," he chuckled.

"That's true. Listen, this may be way too last minute, but I wonder if you and Carter would like to join us at Universal Studios Hollywood tomorrow? It's not that far from Joshua Tree."

He considered. There wasn't anything that he had planned for the next day that couldn't be done another day. It had been a while since they did anything vacation oriented.

"What time did you want to be in the park? I think we could swing that."

"We're thinking ten. We're planning to eat at City Walk for lunch. There's a Buca Di Beppo's there."

"Always with the food, right, babe? I love that about you."

"I don't want to hold you up, Joe. Should we talk later?"

"No, let's finish the arrangements. Are you spending the night there tomorrow night?"

"We are. There's a hotel here. Everything is paid for. There's room for you two to spend the night if you want to. We have a suite."

"I don't suppose you're ready to spend the night with me in front of the kids and your parents?"

"No, I'm not. I'll be torturing us just a little bit with that."

"Not just a little bit, but I forgive you." He considered. *"We'll be there, Dana. Sometimes I forget to slow down. It'll be good for us. And I can meet your parents."*

"That should be interesting. Do you like fast rides?"

"Now there's a loaded question." They relaxed in their easy humor, each of them comforted by knowing that they would be together again soon.

"Should we meet you in the hotel, then, about 9:30 tomorrow morning?"

"Yeah, what room are you in? And Dana, I don't want you to pay for us."

"Nobody's paying for it, Joe. They gave me the room, food vouchers, and the season passes to the

park. It was a gift from the studio. I knew you were gonna bring that up."

"I see."

"We're in room," she laughed *"444 at the Universal Hotel."*

"You're not kidding, are you?"

"Nope."

"This is gonna be fun."

"How can we miss, Joe? We always have fun."

"Babe, you are...I don't even have the words."

"Brilliant? Sexy? Funny? Those are words."

"And so humble." Amazingly, he meant it. She was very humble about what a miracle she was to him. *"So we're set then? We'll see you tomorrow?"*

"Tomorrow," she breathed the word.

Tomorrow she would be introducing her parents to the man she felt she was guaranteed to live out a fantasy with.

Chapter 20

"What do you want to do tomorrow, Carter? Do you have any plans?" Joe took his eyes off the screen House was playing on and tried not to give the surprise away.

Carter chewed the pot pie he had brought home from Kentucky Fried Chicken, vaguely dissatisfied with the way it made him feel. "No plans really. Just riding and working like usual."

Joe considered Carter to be one of the most even tempered people he knew.

"You look good on The Duke. The two of you seem to be getting along better these days."

They were settled in for the night. The work was done for the day. Neither had anywhere they wanted to go or anything they wanted to do.

The living room they ate in was furnished and decorated in a southwestern style that had come with the house. They had made a similar deal with the family they sold their ranch to when they moved here. One thing they had been sure to bring with them was the huge screen TV and the theater quality sound system.

"We came to an understanding. He's a good horse."

Joe nodded, proud that his son was maturing in the way he handled horses. "That's what it takes. I was thinking we could drive out to Hollywood tomorrow morning, go to Universal Studios with everyone. We'll come back Thursday."

The normally slow and steady Carter lit up like a Christmas tree. "Universal Studios?"

"That's the plan."

"With Jason and Dana?"

"And Jenny, and Dana's parents."

Carter nodded. "Great. What time do we need to leave?"

"I figure 6:30." He could sleep in! "I want to give us plenty of time in case we can't find something. I've never been down there."

"Makes sense. What should I bring?"

"Clothes, toothbrush, that sort of thing. We'll stay the night, like I said."

"Was this Dana's idea?" He was animated, his body vibrating with excitement.

"It was her idea." Carter hadn't said much about Dana in the weeks that they had been seeing so much of each other. Apparently he noticed more than he talked about.

"It sounds like something she'd invite us to."

"She's quite a woman. You seem to get along okay with her and Jenny."

Carter was careful with his emotions then. Who knew if she'd be around next month, or even next week? "They're nice."

Joe decided this was a good time to tell Carter that his feelings were safe with Dana. He knew that even if they weren't staying together that Dana would never abandon Carter. And they were, thank goodness, staying together.

"Dana's my girlfriend, you know that, right?"

"Yeah, I figured that out."

"There's more, Carter. Dana's not the kind of person who leaves people behind. She's made it big in her business and she still has all the same friends."

"She doesn't call you. She hasn't called you once since she left." But she had called him. And meant it.

"Dana and I have spoken since she's been gone. We're more than just dating, Carter. We have something permanent here." It's okay to love her, he wanted to say. It sounded too Hallmark to let it pass his lips.

"You mean you're going to get married and all that?"

"I don't know how she feels about marriage,

The Dreaming

Carter, we haven't talked about that. I can tell you that we're going to be together."

Carter took his time thinking about that. Jason was cool, one of the nicest kids at school. He had talked to Carter on the first day, showed him around, and offered him a ride home from the first practice. Jenny was, well, going to have to be like a sister to him, he guessed. She was nice, too. He didn't think they'd ever really talked. Dana was, well, she was nice, he thought. Funny, too.

"I'm okay with that, dad. Not that I guess it would matter. If you're in love you're going to do what you want."

"No Carter, I wouldn't. Seeing how Dana is with you is part of why I fell in love with her. I wouldn't choose a woman who wouldn't treat you the way you deserve to be treated." Again.

Embarrassed, Carter turned back to the TV and the food.

Jason's cell phone vibrated on the night stand again. He had changed it to vibrate after the four phone calls he received from Sue since they had spoken the day before at the Getty. Each time she called she talked about how excited she was that they were together and how she couldn't wait for him to get back. He really hadn't said anything. She didn't seem to expect him to.

Jenny looked over from the table she was sitting at eating breakfast a la room service. "Is that her *again*?"

"Yeah." He was still refusing to talk about it.

He didn't have to say anything. He let the call go to voice mail. Jenny was relieved.

"Do you want some more of this?" Jenny pointed at the food.

"Nah. I'm tired of hotel food."

"Me, too. This wasn't bad though."

"Mom, dad, I've invited Joe and Carter to come with us today. I'm giving them the center room of the suite tonight, too." She couldn't help the fact that she was slightly nervous. She should have told them right away. Now Joe would be walking into the room in about a half hour and their whole day was different. She felt cowardly and insensitive.

George smiled wide, pleased. "I'm happy to hear that, sweet pea. I want to see this man that's got your head so turned around. See what he's all about."

"Dad," she warned.

"I think it's great, Dana. I want to meet him too. Your father will behave." There was a warning in there for him.

"Dana, who is this girl that's calling Jason? Something about it doesn't seem right." Meredith sat at the little dining table sipping coffee.

"I don't know, but I do know that she's new. He hasn't really focused all that much on dating."

George ruffled his paper. "Kid looks like that he's going to have girls burning up his cell phone battery."

Dana heard the pride in his voice. "He's a good kid, dad, isn't he?"

"The best. Did he have a choice?"

There was a knock at the door then.

"Joe, is that you knocking at our door?"
"It's us. Some place you got here, babe."
"It's much better now that you're here."
"You alone in there?"
"No, I'm finishing breakfast with my parents."
"Hmmm."

"I'll get it," Meredith jumped up, beating her husband to the door. He stood just behind her, his fiercest "I'll break you in two if you mess with my little girl" gleam in his eyes.

Dana laughed, shaking her head and calling to the twin's room. "I have a surprise for you. Come in here."

Joe stepped into the room, all six feet of him, wearing tennis shoes and shorts. He hardly resembled the rancher she had come to love. He looked even more like Carter now that he was dressed like him.

"Morning, Mrs. Robin. I'm Joe Jacobs, this is

my son, Carter." He reached up to respectfully remove the hat he wasn't wearing. Laughed to himself. "Mr. Robin." He met the warrior gleam in the older man's eyes with one of his own. It said, "She has two men watching out for her now."

George was instantly satisfied with Dana's new man. Meredith breathed a sigh of relief and looked him over herself. He certainly was handsome, no mistaking that. Handsome enough that she would have worried if George wasn't shaking hands with him enthusiastically.

"Good to meet you, Joe. I've heard some good things about you."

Joe looked past them to Dana, smiling. "I can imagine who it is you've been talking to."

"You'd be surprised," George answered, watching Dana go dreamy eyed.

"Hmmm," he moved to her. There was no way he would be able to greet her without a small, friendly kiss.

"Carter, Joe, hey, when did you guys get here?" Jason burst into the room when he heard their voices.

Carter answered for his dad who seemed to have gone deaf. "About 30 minutes ago. This place is huge."

He pulled Dana into his arms, respectful of the eyes that were on them. "It feels really good to hold you, babe."

"Ummm," she agreed, holding him close, smelling the unique scent of him.

He tipped her chin up for a short kiss, managing to keep his tongue in his own mouth. He was close to blowing all of them off and kidnapping her for some time alone.

She breathed into the kiss, loving that they were together again. She smiled against his lips. "Hi, Joe."

"Yes, well, I think we should get down to the park, don't you?" George cleared his throat, drawing attention away from the steamy greeting.

"Good idea, dad." Dana forced herself out of Joe's embrace. She got as far as one final handhold.

He wasn't letting go.

Meredith saw that Carter's eyes were fixed on the leftover breakfast on the table. "Why don't we take a few minutes to finish breakfast? We have a lot of pancakes and eggs left here. Coffee and orange juice. What are they thinking, Dana? We ordered breakfast for 5, not 50." She shook her head at the waste.

"So that's where she gets it from," Joe commented. He went to hug Jenny and Jason, surprised that he had missed them as much as he had.

"Gets what from?" Dana asked, handing Carter a plate.

"Your aversion to throwing food away. Not that

I disagree, but it really offends you. It only irritates me."

Meredith took it all in. The way Joe had slung a casual arm around Jason for a manly hug, the softer, two armed hug he gave Jenny. Carter and Dana moving comfortably around the table, getting his plate together. They had all the makings of a fine family.

She glanced to her husband, wondering what he was thinking about all of it.

George reseated himself at the table and offered Joe a cup of coffee.

He shook his head. "I already had some. I think I'm going to need my patience for the lines today. They're already huge."

"No lines," George grinned hugely. "We have those VIP things. We go to the head of the line every time."

Chapter 21

"Dude, who is it that keeps calling you?" Carter looked to Jason, frustrated with the number of times the phone vibrated next to him in Jason's pocket. They sat together on a lot of the rides.

"It's..." Jason looked to see where the women of his family were. They had ganged up on him, telling him that he should stay away from a girl that called that much. His grandma had said that letting it go on was like "Punishing himself, on purpose." "Sue Grady, you know the cheerleader?" He kept his voice low when he spotted his mom and grandma standing a little too close.

Carter shook his head. "I don't know her. Why don't you just talk to her?"

"I have, like twice today." And he had no idea what they were talking about anymore. Is this what it was supposed to be like, when a girl really liked you?

"My dad had a couple of women like that before.

He told me he broke it off quick because he didn't want the drama." It was the closest thing to experience Carter had. His only girlfriend had been the girl he took to a Valentine's Day dance just before they moved. He didn't mind too much. She wasn't that interesting to him anyway. She didn't like anything he liked and she was starting to tell him what to do, where to go, and what to wear.

"Does your dad date a lot of women?" Maybe he'd ask Joe about Sue.

"I don't know, kind of, I guess." Carter misunderstood the question and got defensive of Dana. "Dana, uh, your mom, is the only one he's been serious about since the divorce."

Jason raised his eyebrows at Carter. "Really?"

"Yeah, really. He told me they're *permanent*." Carter shook his head at the word. Who said things like that?

Dana caught the tail end of Carter's sentence. He'd told Carter what? That they were permanent?

She looked to where her dad and Joe stood in front of the Nickelodeon playhouse, watching all the kids go crazy throwing water and soft foam balls at each other. They looked envious.

"So, Joe, you look very cozy with my daughter and her kids." George was fairly sure that Joe was well intentioned, but it didn't hurt to have some reassurance. The boy could be turned around about

The Dreaming

what he was really doing.

"I feel very cozy with Dana and the twins." He'd been waiting for this moment. He already knew what to tell Dana's father. And that it was something he hadn't told Dana yet.

"You been married before? To Carter's mother, maybe?" He kept his eyes on the action, his tone anything but casual.

"Yes, I was married to Carter's mother. I'm divorced."

They danced around it a little longer, George wanting assurance that Joe was serious about Dana, Joe curious about where George would go with the questions.

"The wife wants to keep the kids for you two for tonight so you can go out alone, and then take them to Sea World tomorrow so you can have one more day to yourselves. I won't do that for a man who isn't serious about my daughter. Your son doesn't deserve to get jerked around like that. He's a good kid."

This time Joe did chuckle. "I hope I'm as scary as you when Jenny looks serious about a guy."

George felt a well of pride sting his eyes. He was hoping he hadn't missed the mark with Joe and his intentions. He liked the kid. He made his family happy. "I'll help you practice."

"You can put away your sniper rifle, George. I'd

marry Dana today if there was a reason to rush things."

The older man turned away, looking for his wife to tell her they'd be going to Sea World the next day.

"Mom, hold my phone. I don't want it to get wet." Jason emptied his pockets into Dana's hands, barely stopping to be sure anything didn't fall to the ground as he ran from the bucket of water Carter was hunting him with.

"What do you suppose dad's talking to Joe about over there?" Dana chewed her lip, wondering.

"If I know your father, he's trying to scare him off. If he scares, Dana, I hope you'll let him go. It'll hurt less in the long run." She stroked her daughter's arm. "I know you love him."

"He won't scare, mom." Everything about her said she was positive.

"Then what are you worried about?"

"I want them to get along."

"I see. So, Dana, tell me, are you going to encourage that young man to call you mom? He hasn't mentioned his mother once since we met him."

"You're hell on details, mom. No, Carter doesn't mention his mother. Joe's mentioned her once that I can think of." She considered her mother's question. "Carter has a mother, somewhere, so I won't encourage him to call me mom." She turned to her for advice. "Would you?"

Meredith considered it all once again, adding in what she knew now that they had spent hours together playing, the seven of them. "No, I wouldn't for some time, if it was me. Who knows what kind of relationship he could build with his mother, in time?"

She asked her question almost as directly as George had asked his. "Do you want to marry him, Dana? Does he want to marry you? You've got these kids to think of. I trust you not to play house, but what about him?"

Again, Dana knew that they hadn't known each other long enough, strictly speaking, to be having these conversations with anyone, let alone her parents. But she knew most of the answers.

"Mom," she gestured expressively, "we haven't discussed marriage, but I guarantee that no one is playing with anyone's feelings. Joe and I are going to spend the rest of our lives together."

Meredith nodded, satisfied. Then sniffed, knowing that Dana was happier than she had ever seen her.

The phone in Dana's hand vibrated. She glanced at the display. "It's that Sue again. What is that about? Has anyone said anything to you about it?"

"Not only haven't they said anything, but they

won't answer questions about it." And she was worried that Jason had attracted a crazy girl to him.

The impish gleam in Dana's eye had Meredith laughing. "Don't answer it, Dana. You'll start a war."

Joe stood watching the groups, the teens playing in the huge play area, and Dana standing just a little ways from her parents. He supposed George was telling Meredith about his declaration. He felt good having said it.

Standing where he was he was treated to the show of a group of guys, early 20's, he gauged, strolling past Dana and bowing to her, one of them dropping to one knee and reaching for her left hand.

She stepped backwards, laughing and shaking her head. The guy pretended to be disappointed, then having the bright idea of asking for an autograph. This time Dana nodded and signed the paper he offered.

He waited until they cleared away before he walked to her. "Man, but do I have competition."

"What are you gonna do about it?" She teased, cocking her hand on her hip in a sexy pose.

"Your parents have offered to entertain the kids tonight, so that we can go out. I'll be happy to show you what I'll do about it then." He pulled her close. "Can I take you dancing, babe?"

The Dreaming

The phone buzzed in her pocket, vibrating between them.

"You won't need that when I get you alone, babe."

She laughed. "It's not mine. It's Jason's." She turned serious. "I think he has a stalker."

"Really? When did it start?"

"In the last couple of days, from what I can tell. She calls constantly. I don't even know who she is."

"Hmmm. I'll see if he'll talk to me. Maybe it's a guy thing. He doesn't know how to tell her he's not interested or something like that."

"Thanks, Joe." She tried not to notice his hard-on pressing against her side. Clearing her throat she asked, "Did you mean that? My parents are going to make it so we can go out alone tonight?"

"Yeah. I passed my interview with George. He's tough, but I guess with a gorgeous daughter he's had plenty of practice."

"I thought you were having a serious talk over there."

"More serious than any we've had, Dana. But it's good. They're also offering to take the kids to Sea World tomorrow so we can have a day to ourselves. Did you get passes for that, too?"

"Yeah, I did. I didn't think we'd use them. I was going to donate them to a fund raiser for the high school."

"Your folks are great, Dana. No surprise there, I guess."

"They are, aren't they? They were very strict to grow up with, but all in all they really just cared a little too much about some things."

"Again, I can't blame them. You're gorgeous, and sweet. It took that whole 30 minutes the first night at your house for me to drool all over myself. But since I'm a good guy, I took it slow."

Dana looked around them then, pointing at the kids, her parents, his hips thrust into her side. "This is slow?"

"Dana, if all I wanted was sex, it would have been a lot different."

"Yeah, you would have struck out."

He bit her ear in response. "Good. You deserve much more than a horny guy looking to get off."

"Aren't you a horny guy looking to get off?"

"I'm a boyfriend who *is* going to get off, damn it, soon." He growled in her ear, making her wet.

He brushed against her breast, satisfied with the way her nipples pushed through her tank top. "And since I'm a good guy, I'll make sure you get off, too."

"Damn right you will." She gave into the hot kiss they hadn't given each other in a week and a half.

George threw a small bucket of water at them. "You're not married to her yet, Joe."

Chapter 22

"What is this called, Joe?" Dana asked, sitting on his lap at B.B. Kings, panting with sexual heat.

"Torture, or heaven. I'm not sure which one it is at the moment." He stopped himself, again, from edging his fingertips inside her panties and slipping them into her. He knew she was dripping wet.

Her way of thanking him for his restraint was to grind her hips against his hard-on and moan happily.

"Dana, I'm so close to trying to slip it in it's not even close to funny. I'm not wearing anything and I think they could arrest us for what we're already doing." The corner booth he'd found for them was intimately lit. They weren't the only ones taking advantage of the low lighting.

Her expression went serious. "What do we do, Joe? Wait until tomorrow when my parents take off with the kids?"

A waitress walked by, laughingly telling them to get a room.

"You're brilliant," he told her. Then to Dana, "That's what we'll do. Let's step outside and see if they have a room for us at the Universal."

"Joe, we can't spend the night like that," Dana protested, thinking of her parents. She wasn't too old to get a lecture, or to be mortally embarrassed.

"Babe, I'm going to fuck you senseless and then take you back to sleep alone in your suite. When everyone leaves after breakfast, I'll do it again. Then we'll drive home and I'll do it again." He was growling, past the point of frustration, and into agony.

"Who needs romance?" she panted in his ear, ran her tongue down his Adam's apple.

That stopped him. "Ah, Dana. Damn it. You do. I'm not a fucking sailor on leave."

"Could you be one for tonight? I like it." She brushed her fingers over the front of his shorts, outlining the way he stretched the material.

He started walking them back to the tram to get back to the hotel, dialing. He looked into her eyes, wanting to know that she was sure. All he saw staring back at him was the full-sized erogenous zone they had turned themselves into.

"I'm looking for a room for tonight. King or queen is fine. One bed. We'll be there in a few minutes, we're on City Walk." He listened to the hold music where the young voice on the phone had put him while he checked for rooms.

The day had already been one of the most amazing of his life. He'd seen both he and Carter warmly welcomed by Dana's parents, confirming another reason she was the woman he'd been promised so long ago. He'd stopped thinking about that prediction after the second woman he had met in The Dreaming had run, almost screaming, away from him.

"Do we have enough condoms, Joe?" she asked in his ear just as the clerk came back on the line. They heard him laugh before he masked it.

He nodded yes to her and listened again. "We'll take it. Joe Jacobs." He spelled his name and reached for his wallet to get out the card to reserve the room with. Dana's eyes went wide when she heard the price of the room.

He shook his head at her, firmly vetoing the cooling he saw in her body language. He pulled her to the wall, dipping his head to press his tongue to the globes that pushed up out of her tank top when he pulled it low.

"It's only money, Dana, and I haven't spent hardly anything anyway."

She wasn't in a position to argue and she knew it. "Thank you, Joe."

The desk clerk was the same one Joe had spoken to.

He could hide the fact that he was enjoying the kid's envy that he was obviously about to get good and laid, but why try? He hit the jackpot, and he knew it.

"You have room 644." His brown eyes flashed down to Dana's cleavage as he said it.

"Eyes up here," Joe demanded, signing the slip. Guilty, the clerk handed Joe the key card. "Check out is at 10:00 tomorrow."

"Thanks."

"I noticed something about you, Joe. You don't look at other women like that." She'd been watching, curious. He was aggressive with her now, but he had started things off slow between them.

"Why would I look? Have you seen my woman?" He turned her to look in the elevators mirrored panel.

"I mean, not even when I'm not paying attention." She couldn't even explain why she was pushing this point.

"I don't look, Dana." He pressed her front to the smooth, cool panel.

"The way I hear it, all guys look, and we haven't been together for very long." What had taken hold of her, she wondered? She wasn't usually insecure.

Joe decided it was a facts of life moment for the two of them. He guessed she wasn't all that experienced, even after so many years of marriage, and then of dating.

The Dreaming

"There's two kinds of looks, Dana. There's the one I'm giving you that says 'I want to fuck you more than I want to breathe,'" he skimmed his hand under the front edge of her panties for emphasis, stroking her throbbing clit. "Then there's the ones that get a poor sloppy in love guy like me in trouble. Some woman walks by and smiles our way, interested, and I have the stupid urge to smile back. Or a woman walks by in a teeny little mini-skirt, reminds me that I was born male, and my sweet, otherwise sane woman looks at me with murder in her eyes."

He took that moment to share with her what he had already shared with Carter and George. Looking into her eyes he declared, "The second type is the only one you'll ever see out of me, and I'll do whatever I can to make sure that doesn't happen. You're it for me, Dana. There is nothing that any woman, anywhere, has that I want. You're going to be taking care of my urges for the rest of my life. Got it?"

She had needed to hear it, she realized. That's why she had pressed the point. He seemed like such a maverick in so many ways, and in so many ways like the perfect gentleman. She knew what she really had. A delicious blend of both. All to herself.

"Yeah, I get it. It's just that you're so damned good looking, sailor. Makes a girl wonder what you're really after when you've got your hand up her skirt in an elevator on the way to a room you have no intention of sleeping in."

The bell dinged, opening the door to a group of drunk guys coming in from a bachelor party in the second floor ballroom. The banner declared that it was the groom's "Last chance at fun party."

Joe shielded her from their view, straightened her clothes.

Dana laughed. "We must have gone up and back down again."

"Yeah, funny," Joe grumbled. He kept Dana behind him, away from loose tongues and roving eyes.

"You married?" The groom slurred at Joe and Dana.

"Yeah," Joe answered.

"Did you tell the wife if you got too friendly with the stripper at the bachelor party?" He could barely stand up.

Joe moved to give them insurance that he wouldn't barf on them. "I didn't have one."

"What, a bachelor party?"

"Nope."

"She got them locked up somewhere, buddy?"

One of the other guests tried to punch Joe in the arm. He missed and dropped to the floor.

"Yep."

"Idiot," another of them hissed. "She's right

there!"

The sixth floor arrived then, just in time. She didn't think she could hold her laughter anymore.

Joe swiped the key card, opening the room for them.

"You are a strange man sometimes, Joe Jacobs." She shook her head, looking around for a stereo. She wanted music.

"What do you mean?" He was rapidly stripping to his bare skin.

"Making up that story in the elevator." She started a slow strip tease, eyes on him.

"I don't tell stories, babe." He watched her, let her work herself back up to the state he hadn't lost despite the interruption.

"Married, no bachelor party, that story." She flung her bra at him, raising her leg up high on the bed, pulling her skirt up to expose her panties. She moved the satin over, spread her lips open for him.

"It was a glimpse at the future, babe, not a story. Who needs a bachelor party?"

"Ever done it with a stripper, Joe?"

"No, but I'm about to." He grabbed her then, teased beyond his limit. He tossed her beneath him on the bed, sheathed himself in thin latex, moved her panties aside, and slid it home. He focused his hearing on her moans, making sure he wasn't too rough while he took exactly what he wanted. Hot, sweaty, hard sex.

"Joe," she screamed her orgasm, fully satisfied.

"Stay with me, babe. I'm not done yet." He pumped hard, dripping sweat on her in the cold room.

He roared his orgasm, holding the headboard while he shook with it.

He dropped onto her, weak.

She stretched, satisfied for the moment, and heady with his attraction to her.

When his breathing started to sound normal she jiggled out from under him, rolling him to his back.

"Isn't there a porno called the sailor and the stripper?" She stroked his cock, taking the spent rubber from it. She leaned over him, pushing her large breasts together, sandwiching his recovering penis in the middle.

"If there is I think he would say 'suck it, baby. Take it all in. Ah, yeah, that's it, baby.'" He laid back, savoring the feel of her mouth working down his shaft.

"Would he spank her, Joe?" She asked against his steely hard cock, tapping the head with her tongue. She swallowed him deep in her throat, stroking his balls.

He came again, instantly. "Lord, Dana. Where did you hide this nasty side of yours?"

"I didn't think I had hidden it. Did I really?"

She worked her way up his body, settling her pussy over his lips. "Can you guess what I want from you now?"

"You're killing me, babe, but I'm going to die happy."

Chapter 23

Joe woke into The Dreaming, Dana curled naked beside him.

He looked for You, surprised when he didn't find him.

A stranger sat on the edge of the bed that was floating in the air. The sky around them graduated in vertical pastel stripes of green, blue, yellow, pink, orange, and purple.

Joe adjusted the blanket over them to cover Dana's generously curved body.

"No need, friend. I've seen her before. I was her first."

A jealousy Joe had never guessed he was capable of reared forward at the stranger's words.

"She never could get enough. I think I ended up disappointing her."

Seeing the man's contrition relaxed Joe. "I'm Joe." He offered a hand in greeting.

Ever the diplomat, Ben shook his hand.

"Ben Carapelli."

The name didn't surprise Joe. He'd figured as much.

"You know the reason she got so good at cooking healthy food was because of my hypertension and cholesterol. I was only 38 when my ticker gave out on me. She really tried, you know." He brushed an affectionate hand over her hair.

She didn't stir.

Joe's possessive streak rose again, and fell. Technically she was married to this man.

Dana nuzzled her sleepy lips to his neck, smiling. "I love you, Joe." She murmured in her sleep.

"I couldn't do it. I couldn't satisfy her like that. Make her smile like that."

Dana stirred, opening an eye at the voice she thought she'd never hear again.

You appeared instantly beside the bed.

"Ben?" She checked to be sure that the sheet covered her. "Is that really you?"

"Are you asking me?" You asked.

She had to laugh at his expressionless question under the circumstances. "No, it was more rhetorical."

"It's me. This guy, Father Time, is granting my dying wish." Ben looked away from Joe, focusing on Dana. "I didn't know you'd have a, what are you, exactly, to my wife?"

Joe shifted uncomfortably, never thinking he'd hear someone else call Dana "his" wife.

"No offense, Ben," Dana spoke in the silence, "but we're not married anymore. Our vows said 'til death do us part. You're not, well, alive, anymore."

"We'll be leaving those out of our vows," Joe declared, understanding for the first time what those words really meant.

"So you're her fiancé?"

Ben was still dynamic, Dana thought, even in death. Commanding. He wore the suit they had buried him in, navy blue, perfectly tailored, shoes shined to a gleaming black.

"We're in love," Dana said at the same time that Joe answered, "We're soul mates."

Dana stared at Joe, dumbfounded. "Really?"

"Are you asking me?" You asked, monotone.

She turned to him, knowing it was worth a precious question. "Yes, I am." She felt Joe squeeze her fingers under the sheet.

The book and a stand appeared next to the bed. You directed Joe and Dana to place their hands on the cover together to ask the question.

"How do we ask?" She looked to Joe for his input.

"It's not my question, Dana. I already know."

"Did you see it before? Is that how you know?"

The Dreaming

Ben interrupted then. "If I knew about this place when I was alive I would have been invincible."

Joe had nothing to say to that. Dana knew that it was typical of Ben's ambition to consider the possibilities of what he could get from the situation.

"Yeah, Dana, I saw it before, and if I hadn't I would know it here anyway." He placed his hand over his heart.

Dana smiled, satisfied. "Do I still lose a question?" She asked You.

"You used two," he answered in a way that was very direct for You.

"Listen, I came here for a reason." Ben was not fond of wasting time, even in death, when he had all he could ever need. "And it was not to see Dana slobbering over another man. I'm sure you understand, right?" He asked the last to Joe.

Joe nodded.

Ben continued. "I almost feel stupid saying this under the circumstances, but my dying wish was to tell Dana that I'm sorry I didn't treat her better, take her out more, and spend more time with the family." He spread his hands expressively. "So now you know. I hope it means something to you."

"Is it alright with you if I hug him goodbye, Joe?"

"Yeah, babe. I'd say he's suffered enough."

She stood, the sheet wrapping around her like a

toga. "Did you do that?" She asked Joe.

He nodded. *"Hugging him naked is off limits. I'm sure you understand."* He echoed Ben's tone to him.

"Ben," she took his face in her hands, glancing back to see Joe laying proudly naked on the bed, watching.

"Dana," he hugged her close. "You are so beautiful, and doing so great with the kids. He seems good for them, too."

"Are you happy, Ben?"

"In one way. I finally got to tell you that I regretted wasting our life together. Finding out that he's your soul mate, that I could have done without."

"Thank you, Ben, for telling me this. Is there anything you want me to tell the twins?"

She was able to let the regret of staying in her lifeless marriage go. She knew that he had loved her.

"That I love them. That I'm proud of them. Proud of you."

It was an odd privilege for Joe to witness the tender exchange between his love for all time and the man she had borne children with.

"Goodbye, Ben."

"Goodbye, Dana," Ben sobbed the words, fading even as he turned away to hide his tears.

Joe's cell phone alarm rang, waking them in time

to go back to the suite they shared with their kids and her parents before it got too late.

He didn't move, stunned by the enormity of what he had witnessed in The Dreaming.

"Joe?" Dana opened her eyes, testing, not sure what she'd find in his.

"Wow," he answered.

"Wow to which part? Before we slept, or in The Dreaming?" She wondered then why she felt so uncertain about his reaction. This was Joe, and of Joe, she was certain.

He shifted so that he could look directly into her eyes. He knew she felt shaky. Who wouldn't?

"All of it, babe. I'm promising you something right now. I will never take you for granted. I waited too long and went through too much before I found you." He kissed her tenderly, tasting their shared passion on her lips. "Do you want to be my wife, Dana?"

He froze when the thought crossed his mind that maybe she didn't want to get married again.

"I-" she swallowed. "Are you proposing?"

"It looks that way. I didn't plan it, but it just feels right, you know? Like we shouldn't waste a minute of our time together." He felt vulnerable beyond words. She could crush him right now, finish him, with the wrong answer. But he wouldn't give up.

"When?" She asked instead of answered.

"Whenever you want, within reason. I don't want to wait for years." Give me something, babe, his eyes pleaded with her.

She sighed. "I want to marry you, Joe. I do. But-" She laced their fingers together, reached up to kiss him sweetly. "Can you ask me again, later on? When we've all had more time together?"

His heart dropped. "What're we waiting for, Dana?" He knew he sounded miserable. There wasn't anything he could do to stop it. "What I'm asking for is time together. The rest of our lives."

"Joe, please understand, I didn't know you existed a few months ago. You own a ranch and I've barely ridden in years." Her eyes plead right back to his.

"I'll put you on a horse today. Will that do it?" He just didn't understand.

"I've accepted that we're going to spend our lives together. I'm not quite as innocent as everyone seems to think I am. I know that you're everything I want. I just don't want to start setting dates and figuring out how to blend our houses."

He turned away, crushed.

"I'm not saying no, Joe. I'm saying not now."

"Same thing," he muttered.

"Not even close. I think it's time for our first compromise. Do you realize we've never even disagreed? There's magic here, Joe."

He scooted off the bed, looking for their clothes. How had they gone from that, tearing their clothes off in a passionate haze, to her putting him off? He really couldn't see the points she made as anything but a rejection.

"Joe?" She plead, wounded.

Shit, he thought, I'm fucking hurting her. In his pain he didn't know what to do for either of them.

"Babe." He handed her clothes to her. "That was a hell of a striptease."

She knew he was trying, and it comforted her. "How about this, Joseph Anthony Jacobs. How about you promise to marry me in a year and a half? That way we'll start making plans in six months. Unless you're scared," she clucked like a chicken, trying to lighten their mood to what was normal for them.

He laughed at that, shoulders shaking, genuinely amused. He shrugged into the black shirt he had brought for tomorrow. His tank top wasn't as nice as Dana's so he'd gone back to the room to change before they went dancing.

"What's that called?" was his answer.

"A promise, Joe. I can even wear a promise ring if that's what we want."

"So you'll be wearing my ring?" He narrowed his eyes, looking for a catch.

"Yes, Joe. It's like I said, I want to marry you, be a stepmother to Carter, your wife, everything that comes with it. Just not yet."

He shook his head again. "What's the difference, Dana? If you put my ring on now and marry me in a year and a half, or you put my promise ring on and marry me in a year and a half?"

She laughed, relieved that they felt more like themselves again. "When you put it that way, there's no difference."

He came all the way back to himself then, knowing that she meant it. "I know one difference. You get three rings that way, instead of two. Is that why the whole promise thing was made up? For extra jewelry?" He teased. He was close, he sincerely hoped, to being engaged to the love of his life. The other part of his soul. And he wanted it more than he had ever wanted anything.

She threw a pillow at him, hoping it would hit him with a little of the frustration she was feeling when he dug in his heels and decided that she was just trying to say no to him in a nice way.

"Put your clothes on, Dana. I have something to ask you. Get the answer right this time, okay? Then we'll go sneak in and hope we don't wake your parents." He shook his head at their strange situation.

How could she resist him? She knew that he

would never take them lightly, never take her for granted. He would always treasure what they shared.

"Where are my panties?" she asked, zipping into her skirt.

"I don't think they made it. I remember something tearing." He smiled widely, remembering that he made her scream out each of her orgasms a few short hours ago.

"Then this is all I have to wear."

"It's cool, babe. All bad girls walk around without panties at least some of the time." They groomed themselves in the mirror, side by side.

"What do you know about bad girls?" She demanded, only half teasing.

"Only what you taught me and what's in the movies." He played innocent.

"I'm not a bad girl, Joe. You can't stretch it that far."

"Babe, you've done plenty of bad girl things to me. I've seen the movies. I know what I'm talking about."

"Give me one example."

"Are you trying to end up back in bed, and not engaged to me?" he accused playfully.

"Joe," she looked vulnerable, purely an act. "I'd like to know."

He held her shoulders, looked into her eyes. He

snorted, then dropped to his knee. "Will you be my bad girl forever and ever?"

"If you tell me one bad girl thing I did." She raised her foot to his shoulder, giving him an enticing view of her bare mound.

"I'd say this qualifies, wouldn't you?"

"What?" she asked, all innocence.

"Dana," he shook his head, laughing. "I'd like to be able to remember proposing, and you saying yes, without getting turned on."

"Why?"

"You know, I'm not sure at the moment. Just humor me, please. After all, you broke my heart once tonight already."

She dropped down to hold him, knowing he meant it. "Did I really, Joe? I'm sorry. Yes, I'll marry you next January."

"I don't plan to repeat this, so listen up." His voice went gritty. "Thinking you didn't want me hurt worse than anything I've ever experienced, including finding out that Beth was having a two year long affair."

"Goodness, Joe. Why didn't she just end it?"

"She didn't want to. She wanted to go on being married to me and sleeping with him. Her logic was that it had been going on for so long it was working in some twisted way. I ended it."

"Was she sleeping with both of you?"

The Dreaming

"You have to know that it wasn't like what we have. It never was. She was still acting like she loved me, including sleeping with me."

"I'm so sorry, Joe." She felt the pain of it, horribly.

"I'm not. I'm engaged to a gorgeous bad girl with a mouth that can say 'goodness, Joe,' and 'suck it, I want to come in your mouth,' with the same passion. It's more than worth the pain of getting over someone who didn't blink an eye at leaving Carter behind." He cupped the back of her head in his hand, pressed his forehead to hers as he shared his heartfelt truth.

It stunned her that anyone could give them up, treat them so carelessly.

"I could never do that, Joe. I could never cheat or hurt Carter. I'm so sorry you misunderstood when I really was just asking for more time."

"Why are we sitting on the floor? We've got five hotel rooms full of furniture." He helped her up, held her face tenderly in his hands. "I know, Dana, babe, that you could never do that."

While she had him in his tender mood she informed him that he would be the one to tell her dad that they were engaged.

"It's already done."

"It is not." She gaped at him.

"Close enough. I told him I would marry you

today," he glanced at his cell phone. "Make that yesterday. He didn't even want to shoot me after that."

"He got tougher after Ben. He thinks he let me down by encouraging our marriage."

He nodded his understanding as the pieces clicked for him. "That's why he was so tough with me. He knew you were in love with me and he wanted to make sure I didn't hurt you by stringing you along."

"As my first act as your fiancée, I think you should ask my parents to come riding at the ranch before they go home to Arizona. Let them get to know you better."

They were on the fourth floor now, creeping toward their other rooms.

"Done." He pulled her close for their last kiss until the day officially began. "I love you, Mrs. Jacobs to-be."

"Mmmm," she started to deepen the kiss. He pulled away. "Not now, bad girl, but definitely later."

Chapter 24

Dana found herself in a room full of shadowy figures. They were sitting in rows as far as her eye could see in any direction.

She turned to the shadow beside her, surprised that it reminded her of Ivy from New York.

"Ivy?" She asked. The shadowy figure shimmered beside her. It seemed excited.

A cloud of gold dust blew over all of them. Its effect was very relaxing.

All of the figures around her sat in their chairs.

Dana did the same, sensing that it was safe, and not knowing what to do instead.

You stood at the podium on the stage.

That was her signal. That was when her mind registered that she was in The Dreaming.

Another wave of colored mist engulfed them then, this time a soft pastel pink. It smelled like roses.

The room around her was different than anything

she had seen yet in The Dreaming. There was no beginning or end to anything. There was no floor to stand on, yet they weren't floating. They were simply there.

"Rose, her name is going to be Rose." She could clearly hear the shadowy figure that reminded her of Ivy. "I'm having a girl." She squealed excitedly.

"Joe?" Dana called. He didn't answer. Nothing changed anywhere around her. "Joe?" She tried again.

"What?" He walked to her bedside. He had been sitting with her parents in the center room of the suite when he heard her call him in his mind the first time, then out loud the second time. He'd excused himself to go to her.

"Where are you? I can't tell which one is you."

She lay curled in sleep, holding her pillow. It would be so easy to slip in with her, but their day was already complicated enough with the announcement of their engagement.

"Babe," he stroked her hair, her arms, gently. "You're dreaming." He understood then that she was in The Dreaming, looking for him.

She came awake slowly, for the second time ever in Joe's presence. Her eyes fluttered open.

Meredith came in behind him. She knew they'd stayed out until the early morning hours. She also noticed that they didn't look like they were about to jump each other like they usually did.

"Rise and shine, sleeping beauty." George came in behind his wife, curious. He thought it was really odd that Dana had called out to Joe in her sleep.

"Dad? Mom? Joe? What are all of you doing in here?" She looked to Joe. *"Did you tell them?"*

He leaned down for a chaste kiss. *"I asked for George's permission. He gave it. I thought we'd wait until everyone was awake to announce it."* Aloud he said, "You were dreaming. You called me. I was in there," he pointed, "having coffee with your parents."

Facts slowly slid into place. "I get it. I was dreaming. What a night."

"No kidding. Those boys can eat," George announced proudly. "If you're alright, we'll leave you alone to get dressed." He shooed his wife and Joe out of the room, craftily closing the door behind them.

"Sweet pea?"

"Yes, dad?" She was glad she was wearing pajamas.

"Do you want to marry him? If you don't, I'll help you out of it. I know his heart's set, but I want you to be sure." He was ready to run Joe off if she wasn't 100%.

"Dad." She got off the bed to hug him. "Thank you for that, but have you met Joe? Why wouldn't I want to marry him?" She sighed happily. The full import of the conversation hitting her.

"He's pushy," George grumbled.

"It's a wonder we're not related."

"I know you love each other, sweet pea, but you don't know each other. It takes love and a whole lot more to go the distance like your mother and I have. You haven't even met his parents yet."

"Dad, we know what we need to know." How could she tell him about all they did and saw in The Dreaming?

He watched her for a few silent minutes. If she started anxiously selling him on the idea he'd find a way to keep it from happening so fast.

She watched him right back.

They started laughing like two loons.

"What's going on in there, babe?"

"My dad's trying to scare me off of marrying you."

"He could give lessons," he laughed. *"I passed twice. You can do it, too. There's Eggs Benedict out here for your reward."*

"Had enough, dad? Did Grandpa Carson do this to you and mom?" She went to her bathroom to make herself presentable for breakfast. For the luxury of staying two nights in the same hotel room she had unpacked her toiletries instead of leaving them in the bags.

The Dreaming

He thought back. "No, they thought she'd never get married. Handed her to me on a silver platter."

He watched her put her robe over her pajamas. "You're every bit as gorgeous as your mother, and smart with it. He's a lucky son of a gun." He crooked his arm to escort her into the center room of the suite.

Everyone was up, filling plates and lounging where they could be together to eat.

"Morning, everyone," she greeted.

Jason's cell phone vibrated. Dana couldn't hold back her laughter. "Does she sleep?"

"Not much," he grumbled.

"I'd turn my phone off at night, then," Joe advised. "She leaving you messages?" He made it easy, respectful, for Jason to answer.

"Uh huh, lots of them." He poured orange juice. "The food here rocks."

"I think it's the best hotel food we've had." Meredith helped Jason shift the talk away from his problem.

"What did you guys do last night?" Dana motioned to her parents and the kids.

"A lot," Carter answered. "We bowled, went to the arcade, saw a band, and ate at the Hard Rock Cafe. I think I saw Katy Perry get out of a limo."

"It wasn't her," Jason argued.

"Are you a bowler, Joe?" George asked.

"Carter didn't tell you? It was all there was to do in Walnut if you didn't want to sit in a bar and drink every time you went out."

"He said he bowled a lot. Didn't mention you," Meredith answered. She plunged to the heart of it. "What did the two of you do last night?"

Chapter 25

Dana hugged her mother from behind, bending to adjust to her seated height. "You know?" she whispered.

"Of course," she laughed. "Go ahead, tell them."

Joe answered. "We went to B.B. Kings and danced for a while." *"You ready, babe?"*

"You can tell them about the engagement. Anything else I would have to deny flat out."

Joe walked to her, put an arm around her waist. He cleared his throat, looking around the room. Dana was the only one still in pajamas.

On instinct they all turned to look at him.

"I asked Dana to marry me. She accepted."

"Really? That's awesome!" Jenny jumped up and ran to them to share congratulatory hugs.

Meredith sniffled. George went to get her a tissue, and grabbed one for himself.

Carter smiled, shyly rising to hug Dana. "Congratulations."

"So you'll have me?" Dana asked him.

He didn't have the words but the look in his eyes said that he was very happy to welcome her into his family.

Jason was the last to respond, trying to put it all together. "When?"

"Excellent question," George approved.

Dana rushed in before Joe could. She had thought of something after they parted. Something that mattered a lot to them. "I was thinking about April 4th. I wonder what day of the week that is?"

"That's a surprise to me," Joe murmured to her.

The teens had their phones out. "It's a Saturday," Jason announced.

"Can I have a minute with you, Jason?" Joe walked to him. He'd have to be blind not to notice that the teen wasn't thrilled with the news.

"Yeah," Jason bounded to the next room, anxious to talk it out.

Joe followed more slowly, getting ready to come to terms with another gatekeeper.

"Jason-"

"Why? Why do you want to get married?" He faced the stronger, bigger man, fiercely.

"Because we love each other. We want to be a family."

"Sure," he said it sarcastically. He believed that they had the hots for each other, that they got along, but love? They didn't even know each other. There had to be a reason for getting married so fast.

Joe held his temper. "Is there some reason you don't believe that we love each other? Or is it that we want to be a family?"

"What's the hurry?"

"Well, that's three for three." Joe laughed to break the tension for himself and for Jason. "I've been explaining that for hours now. The hurry is that we've waited long enough to be happy together. We're old enough to know when we have something extraordinary. Something that will last forever. Your mom and I are both marriage and family people, but there's no reason to waste time confirming for everyone else what your mom and I know."

When Jason didn't respond he continued. "I'm trying to understand how you must feel. I never saw this in my life. My folks are still married."

Jason remained silent.

"Is there something else you'd like to ask me? I'd really like to have your blessing. It matters to me that you're with us on this."

That broke it open for Jason. He knew that he mattered to Joe. That they all did. He held a hand out to shake.

Joe took the hand, glad they were back on even ground. "We're cool?"

"Yeah. Congratulations." He was embarrassed by how long they'd stood there. He hoped everyone would leave him alone about what they had talked about.

"Thank you. I always intend to do right by you, your mom, and your sister. I want you to know that. Now, should we go out there and have some more breakfast?"

He watched, wanting assurance that he really did have his blessing. He opened his arms in invitation.

Jason swung his arm up around Joe's shoulders in a cool guy hug. Joe caught the little sniffle Jason tried to hide.

"Let's go then." Joe held the door open to let Jason pass through.

"I passed my third interview," Joe announced.

George laughed so hard he spewed coffee out of his nose.

Jenny jumped back, checking for splatters. "Eww."

Dana went to them, holding their gazes. "Everything okay?"

"Yeah, mom. I forgot to say congratulations to you both. I really do hope you'll be really happy together." He kept his tone low in his embarrassment.

"It's okay, Jase. You're entitled to some time to get used to it." She looked into the eyes that he had inherited from Ben, reassuring him that she understood that he could take the time he needed to adjust to having Joe as a stepfather.

"No, it's cool. I just want breakfast."

She knew that he meant it, and that not all of Jason's unusually suspicious mood had to do with the surprise engagement.

"It's all here, George. Keys, maps, and here's some food money for the trip." Joe tried to push the money into George's closed hand.

"Joe, it's all handled, like it was here. You just enjoy your day to yourselves. If you're going to call yourself my daughter's fiancé you better get a ring on her finger."

George made his expectations for how he wanted Joe to spend the day clear.

"How did she stay single for so long? Did you scare them all off?" Joe shook his head at George's playful, but no less commanding suggestion.

The older man stopped laughing. "Joe, her marriage was a sham. He didn't appreciate her. I'd say *he* scared her off getting close to anyone. You're the first man we've even heard about since Ben died. Maybe that can help you understand why we're cautious about the fast engagement."

"I've already sworn a blood oath that I'll take care of her, George," Joe soothed. "If you want to take some more skin off my hide you can do that tonight."

George held his hands up in the opulent lobby, surrendering. "Alright, alright, I'm satisfied. And *you* asked *me*, remember?" George felt his bond to Joe grow. "You should know about her marriage."

"I do, George. She knows about mine, too." He changed the subject, touching the keys in George's hand. "Those kids are good drivers. Let them help out. Makes them feel good."

Dana smiled to her mother when they overheard Joe's suggestion to let the teens help with the driving. "He's already trying to take care of you guys."

"I'm happy for you, Dana. Did I forget to mention that?" Meredith hugged her goodbye.

"It got lost in the commotion. Now go." If Dana let it happen they would be red eyed and weepy once again.

Joe and Dana waved them all off, standing there with a big pile of luggage and their own long drive ahead.

Chapter 26

"Okay, help me. What do I do about this?" Jason asked Jenny, pointing at his buzzing phone.

"Tell her that you're not interested? Or that you already have a girlfriend?"

"She doesn't listen to anything I say." He answered helplessly.

They were finally back home, settling back into their normal schedules. They both had to work again starting Monday.

Their grandparents were staying a couple more days with them to visit Joe at the ranch.

The adults sat in the living room, relaxing for the first time together.

Peaches and Cream enjoyed having so many feet to lounge on, and so many hands to pet them. Their adventure at Sunny Skies Stables had been good for them. They had spent their days with Joe and Carter, trailing behind them as they worked and cared for the horses, and sleeping in their beds at night.

Dana admired her engagement ring glittering icily on her left hand.

"That's one pretty ring you picked out, babe. It looks great on you." Joe turned her hand, watched the sparkle.

"I'm beat." George yawned and stretched. "How about a nap, Meredith? We'll be fresh for our first look at Joe's ranch tomorrow morning."

"I admit I could use a nap, too. We've had a busy couple of weeks." She lounged back on Dana's favorite reading couch, gathering the energy to go into the guest room. She launched herself deliberately off the couch. "If we aren't up for dinner you just leave our food in the fridge, Dana. No waiting around for us to eat with you guys." She turned to Joe. "We'll see you tomorrow."

"I'm looking forward to it," he answered truthfully. He enjoyed himself with the Robins.

George and Meredith took their time strolling to the guest room, glad they didn't have anything more pressing to do than visit with their family for the next couple of days before they flew back home.

Joe took the moment to cuddle with Dana, to share a few more kisses while they were alone. "I'm spoiled now, babe. We had time alone two days in a row. Your folks are very thoughtful."

"Mmmm. They are very thoughtful." She swallowed him in the kiss, stroking his shoulders and hair. Her breasts swelled with arousal.

"Uh hmmm." Jason cleared his throat. "I, uh, need your help. Sue isn't leaving me alone. I told her I wasn't looking for a girlfriend, and that it wasn't working out between us. It didn't change anything." He spread his hands helplessly.

"Hmmm," Joe considered. He angled his body to shield Dana's chesty reaction to their kiss. "I think you should change your number and ask your friends to keep it to themselves. By the time school starts it'll be history. That's my take."

"What kind of messages does she leave?" Dana wanted to know, concerned that things may have gone much too far in a few short days.

"Nothing weird." Jason shrugged. "The same thing over and over. We'll go there, we'll do that. That sort of thing."

"Do you think she knows you're back?" The messages were weird enough for her to get involved.

"I didn't tell her. No, I don't think she knows."

Jenny came in through the kitchen from the pool.

"Oh, good. I wanted to ask what you know about Sue?" Dana invited Jenny's input.

She looked to Jason apologetically. "Sorry, Jase, I have to tell them. I stay faaar away from her. She's trouble." She plopped down on the floor to pet the dogs she'd missed while they were gone. Jenny's bond with the dogs was the closest by far.

"You're wet," Dana scolded.

"Oops, sorry." She gathered her towel and went to stand in the doorway on the tile.

"What do we need to do, Jenny? Would changing his number be enough?" Joe was impressed with his stepdaughter-to-be. She had a level head on her shoulders.

"Could be. The less she knows about you, the better. If she doesn't know you're back, where you work, or where you live, it could fizzle out."

"I'm hoping. I'll start with changing my phone number. Thanks, guys." His gratitude was for more than the advice. It was for being treated respectfully when he had ignored their concern in the first place.

"No big." Jenny answered, then wandered into her bathroom to shower.

"I'd love to stay, but our adventures these last couple of days have taken a toll on my workload at the ranch," Joe said regretfully. "You're welcome, of course, to come with your folks when they come out tomorrow."

"I'd like that, Joe. We'll only stay for a couple of hours ourselves. I have to get started on the next book and my parents should have a chance to rest whether they think they need to or not." She walked him to the door.

"I'm going to skip tomorrow, Joe. I want a day to sleep in and do nothing." Jason waved his goodbye from the dining room table.

Dana laughed. "What do you call today? I didn't see you until almost noon. That means you've been up for, what, three hours?"

"It doesn't count. I didn't turn my phone off." He held up his now silent phone. "I'm telling my friends to call me on the house phone until I get a new cell phone number and to keep it to themselves."

She and Joe nodded, feeling better now that Jason was taking action.

"What are you going to do, babe?" Joe asked when she walked him out the front door.

"I have no idea. Isn't that wonderful? I have no plans until we come out to your place tomorrow." She breathed a big sigh of relief at her freedom.

The house was in perfect shape. Brittany had come by while they were gone to bring the mail into the house and water everything. She'd cleaned once while they were gone since there wasn't anyone there the rest of the time for the usual weekly visit.

"I've got food in the freezer for tonight so I won't cook until tomorrow. I'm thinking about taking a swim and then a nap." She lounged against the side of his truck, enjoyed watching him.

"You should do that, babe. Relax. You make it look easy but you must need some time off to yourself." He leaned on the truck next to her, a hand stroking down her arm.

Her mind strayed, as it usually did, to what she and Joe had done every chance they had the day before.

"Don't go there, babe. I really can't stay. Besides, you have a full house right now." He still leaned in for a steamy kiss, unwilling to resist.

"I can fantasize, can't I?" She purred against his lips.

"There's very little I wouldn't give you for the asking, Dana. If you want to fantasize about us, go right ahead. Just remember that I might be with people when you do. It could get embarrassing." Like now, he thought. He was sporting a hard-on that would definitely be noticed.

"It amazes me, Joe, how much we affect each other. I'll be respectful of that."

"Of course you will. Your respect goes bone deep." He gathered her closer. "I'll see you tomorrow, love."

"I like when you call me love. It's sweet." Dana stepped away, putting the distance between them that she knew she needed to let him go without pulling him back into the house with her or getting into the truck to go with him.

Dana drove her parents over to Joe's ranch the next day, glad for the slight break in the heat. It was only

90 today and not too humid with it.

"How did you and Joe meet again?" Meredith asked, her wide eyes taking in the gorgeous horses in the arena.

Dana followed her gaze and saw Joe working a colt he was training for a client. She thought his name was Gentleman Jim.

"Carter and Jason were on the track team together. Jason gave Carter a ride home on a test day to eat with us and Joe came to pick him up." She sighed at their romantic story.

Meredith joined her in the sigh.

"I haven't been on a horse in years," George noted. He'd worn the only boots he owned, jeans and a polo shirt for the visit.

"I still go riding once a month with Donna. It makes me feel so free. She swears I'm helping her keep Dusty in shape. I think it's the other way around!" Meredith noticed how well kept everything was. The grounds were impeccable.

"Joe has a few horses to choose from for you to ride today, mom. He says he wants me to ride Moonlight. She's seven years old and very gentle. Perfect for a beginner." Dana parked in front of the house, which now seemed to be her spot.

Joe smiled and waved them over.

"This is a big place you've got here, Joe. It must cost a fortune to keep the barns cool in the summer heat." George looked at the practical bottom line of things.

"It would if it wasn't all solar powered. If it wasn't already set up that way I would have done it myself." He reached up and tipped his hat to the ladies in greeting. "Morning."

Dana walked into his arms for a hug and a little kiss.

"Why do I always want to jump you, Joe?"

"Because I'm lucky."

"I mean it. I've never been this...attracted to anyone before. I, it sounds corny, but I crave you."

"We're meant for each other, love. It's fate." He turned slightly more serious. He wanted to flirt but it seemed she was looking for an answer.

Fate was a vague concept to Dana. One she needed to think more about.

"I'm hoping I can get all of us out for a little ride today. This lovely woman is going to be a rancher's wife so it would be good for her to get comfortable with the horses." Joe led the colt to the bigger arena to enjoy roaming in the relatively cool day.

"I'm ready to give it a try," Dana agreed. "I'd like to ride Moonlight. She looks calm."

"She is, and she'll grow for you, too. When you get more experienced you can take her out for a fast ride. She loves it." He urged them into the arena to meet the horses.

The Dreaming

"My mom has a lot of riding experience. At least with her you don't have to teach so much."

"I've never ridden an Arabian, though. Donna raises Tennessee Walkers. I mentioned today to her and she said to expect some differences in the gait."

Meredith's eye was seasoned enough to know that every horse in front of her was very well cared for.

Joe nodded. "Tennessee Walkers are really a pleasure to ride. The gait on these guys is different, but I'm sure you'll handle it just fine." He brought Sunshine to her. "I think you and Sunshine will get along well."

Meredith greeted the horse, rubbing her neck affectionately and smiling. Sunshine stood for the interaction, her eyes shining with intelligence.

"I mean this in the nicest way, Joe, but how smart are horses? She looks like she knows a thing or two." George marveled at the world he was stepping into.

"They're incredibly smart, George. My new stallion, Medallion, would be a hell of a gambler if he could hold the cards. He's incredibly quick and crafty. He's becoming my favorite to ride. In fact," he turned to Dana, "I thought I'd put you up on him, in front of me, for a little bit today. I wouldn't let you ride him on your own for a while yet, but I'll be guiding the whole thing. I just want to share the feeling with you." He was hungry to share everything with her.

Dana nodded. "I'd like that. So what will you be doing for dad?"

"Moonlight, same as you. I don't expect either of you to spend a lot of time in the saddle on your first day. Mostly I thought you'd get to know them, see how to saddle them and rub them down after a ride. Very basic stuff."

Meredith approved his approach and Sunshine. "She is wonderful, Joe. I appreciate the chance to ride her."

"Let's get her and Moonlight out here. Medallion's already in the barn. We'll saddle everyone and take a short walk around, see what everyone does. For this first time, George, I'll have Dana in front of me. If it's not working for you you'll be able to dismount right away."

"I feel fine with that, Joe. I've had experience with them, just not in a long time." He took Moonlight's reins and led her to the barn alongside of Meredith and Sunshine.

Moonlight nuzzled close to Dana's hair, snorting.

Joe laughed, happy. "If the two of you hit it off I'd like to give her to you. I think she's the one for you."

Chapter 27

In the cool of the barn Joe showed everyone where the tack was and how to saddle each horse.

Meredith helped George while Joe helped Dana get comfortable with Medallion's size.

"There's one more thing for you, love." Joe reached into the supply locker and pulled out a box, handed it to Dana.

Dana took the box, flustered. "What's this about?"

"Open it. You'll see." He leaned against the stall, enjoyed the surprise on her face.

The white box contained a ladies black cowboy hat.

She laughed at her memory of him saying he wanted to make love to her in a cowboy hat.

"Let's put that on you." Joe positioned the hat on her head. He nodded. "Looks good, love."

"I don't have a mirror to see myself in."

"You look better than my wildest fantasy," Joe

assured her.

"Oh!" Meredith exclaimed. "I want a picture of you wearing that hat. Doesn't she look pretty, George!"

"She does. It looks right on her, too," he said, considering. The speed of the engagement was something he could do without, but he had to admit that everything that was happening seemed to fit them all perfectly. Not just him and Meredith, or Joe and Dana, or the kids, but all of them.

They walked the horses outside. Joe helped George mount Moonlight. Meredith confidently mounted Sunshine. Joe mounted Medallion and pulled Dana up in front of him on the saddle. He settled his arms around hers, pulling her back into him. She sighed with the contact.

"I know, love. It feels good to hold you like this."

They walked the horses around to get the feel of it. Joe saw that everyone was in good shape and suggested that Meredith take Sunshine a little faster. They would follow her. He assured them all that the trail was well kept and they'd only be out for a little while on it.

"I've never seen anything like Medallion, Joe. He's breathtaking."

"All the mares agree with you. He's a stud." He kept a careful eye on George, satisfied that he was remembering quickly what he had done on a horse in the past.

They walked the trail a short way, then headed back. Joe put Medallion back in his stall and guided George's dismount off Moonlight. "Let's get you up on Moonlight for a few, Dana. I'd like to see what the two of you do together."

Meredith took Sunshine around the property, in close view of what Dana was doing with Moonlight. "George, go get the camera and take some pictures?"

George followed his wife's request. He wanted the pictures, too. She looked good on Sunshine.

"Looks like we have more reasons than before to visit you, Dana. Your mother looks like she's in love with that horse."

"They do look right together," Dana agreed. She was astride Moonlight, and thrilled at how comfortable she was with her. They moved together like they knew each other. "Did the sale hold?"

"Yeah, they'll be picking her up next week. No worries, though. I'll always have plenty of horses for your folks to ride."

George snapped the pictures, pleased with the camera Dana had given him for the trip. His daughter knew her electronics.

Joe nodded at the way Dana and Moonlight moved together. She might feel like he was being overly generous to give her the mare, but for him, giving a gift to Dana was like giving one to himself, she appreciated everything so much. He couldn't imagine a better owner for Moonlight.

Meredith sidled up to Dana and Moonlight. "Did I hear him say that he sold Sunshine?"

Dana marveled at how natural it felt to be there on Moonlight, and the way that she and Sunshine got along so well.

"Yes, he did. He's happy with where she's going."

"Did you name Sunshine, Joe?" Meredith inquired.

"No, she came to me as a three year old. The former owner, a boarder at my old place, couldn't take care of her very well. I offered to buy her, work with her. She was a little problematic when I first got her. She needed more attention than she was getting and started to develop little idiosyncrasies because of it."

"I would never know," Meredith sounded impressed. "You really know your stuff, Joe."

"Thanks." He shrugged it off.

"What about Moonlight, Joe? What's her story?" Dana wanted to know.

His face softened. "Moonlight was born on a really bright night. The moon was the whitest I've ever seen it. I knew there was something special about her the moment she was born."

The Dreaming

"You delivered her?" George was more impressed with his daughter's choice as he listened.

"Yeah, I delivered her." He reached to pat her affectionately. "What do you think, love? Is she the horse for you?"

"I can't imagine liking any horse more, Joe."

"In time you'll come to love her. She already loves you."

"Thank you, Joe, for everything."

"Not so fast. I expect you to help me put lunch together for your folks."

"It just so happens I know a little something about that."

Chapter 28

Dana listened to the days messages on Jason's old phone number days after Jason had stopped responding to Sue's calls. There were only four, which was down from six or seven, depending on the day. Apparently Sue was camping with her family and couldn't always get phone reception.

They were typical to what she'd been hearing. Dana was truly puzzled as to why the girl kept calling when she didn't get a response. There were messages that clearly showed that the girl didn't care if Jason listened to them or not.

Dana found the whole thing creepy.

She saved the messages as she had each day so that if anything needed to be heard by someone else she'd have it. She wondered if the girl's parents knew about her fixation?

Dana's cell phone rang, making her jump, and laugh. The caller ID showed Lucy Shannon.

"Hey, Lucy!"

The Dreaming

"You sound happy."

"You do, too. How are you?" Dana glanced at the clock to see how much time she could spend with Lucy on the phone.

"I'm super dee duper. So, you made a heck of a splash with 'Dana Cooks Healthy Food for Kids'. Congrats!" Lucy bubbled into the air. Her Bluetooth caught the conversation for her and sent it to Dana while she sat in front of her keyboard looking at her schedule of when she would be out Dana's way for another working lunch.

"Yep, I did. Did you get your copy in the mail?"

"Yes." The bubbles stopped while Lucy choked back her tears. "Thank you for dedicating the book to me, D. It's really...special."

"*You're* really special, Lucy. You're the best friend I've ever had."

"Well, good, then you won't mind meeting me at this new restaurant in Riverside on Thursday. It's one of those health food store slash tea shop slash hippy hangouts. You'll love it. What I've seen so far isn't too scary. You know how the food can be hit and miss with those set-ups."

"Let me see, Thursday," Dana checked her calendar to confirm what she remembered. Yes, it was clear. As she opened her mouth to ask for the details she thought of Joe. She stretched the silence with Lucy to ask if he would like to go. She wanted them to meet. She wanted to announce their engagement and ask Lucy to be her maid of honor.

"*Joe?*"

"*I was just thinking of you, love. How are you?*" *His tone held all the warmth he felt for his love.*

"*Really? I'm great, Joe. I want to know if you're free on Thursday? I'm having lunch with my best friend. We'll be meeting in Riverside.*"

"*Thursday? Hmmm.*" *He thought over his schedule.* "*Sure, we can do that. Where's Riverside?*"

"*It's a good drive from here, Joe. We'll be gone about half the day,*" *she warned.*

"*I'll be trapped in a car with you for hours? Sign me up.*"

"*Awe. I'll talk with you soon, Joe. I love you.*"

"*Love you too. Moonlight says hi. She misses you.*"

"Lucy? Can I bring Joe with me? I'd like you to meet."

Lucy came back to attention, wondering if the delay in Dana's response was her talking to the mysterious Joe. She shrugged it off as a no, since she hadn't heard anything.

"Oh, yes, do bring Joe." Lucy's tone held a protective edge.

Dana laughed, thinking that Joe was in for another interview if she didn't head it off now.

"Lucy, he's already passed inspection. My parents even like him." She knew that would perk Lucy up.

"He met your parents?" She narrowed her eyes. "Are you two getting serious?"

"Not getting, are. You'll love him, Lucy. He's gorgeous and wonderful."

"Does he have a brother?"

Dana laughed with Lucy about the eternal hope she had that she would find a great guy through a fix-up. "No, two sisters."

"Does he like health food? What am I asking, of course he does if he's hooked up with you." Lucy pressed send on the computer so that Dana had all the information for The Shake Shack.

"He likes my food because it's good. He's leery of health food in general. If it's terrible, he'll tell you." Joe didn't pull punches.

"Perfect. I'm going to have to run now, D. I e-mailed all the info to you. See you then!"

"Perfect," she echoed.

Tuesday was Jenny's first six hour work day of the summer. Lavender was talking about the upcoming party, who would be there, how cool she thought it was going to be. She was enthusiastic about a new guy her roommate was hanging out with.

Jenny took the opportunity to break the news to her that she wasn't going while they were alone in the store. A lot of the time they had a couple of Lavender's friends there during the day when the owner was out.

"I'm sure you're going to have a great party. I found out that I can't make it." She braced for Lavender's reaction, not sure what she would say.

It's You was a basic fashion store. They had three clearance racks, jewelry stands near the counters, rounds full of clothes for young men and women. They carried trendy make-up and fragrances. Lots of t-shirts. Few of the items they carried retailed for more than $25.00. None were more than $40.00.

"Why not?" Lavender's tone was casual.

"I have some stuff to do with my mom that night. She's working on a new book." It wasn't entirely truthful, but she knew that she could make it that way. Her mom was always ready to work on her new ideas, and she loved it when Jenny was interested.

"Can't it wait? Or can't you do it earlier? I was really counting on you to be there."

Lavender sounded so friendly she couldn't believe there was anything wrong there. But a promise to her mom was a promise to her mom. She'd keep it. She couldn't think of another time that she had asked her for such a thing. Jason hadn't listened when she told him to look out for Sue because he couldn't see what she saw. If her mom was wrong time would tell and she could hang out with Lavender then.

"No, sorry. We're just busy right now." Jenny kept her hands and eyes busy hanging the new pajamas that came in. They had big ducks, pigs, or cows all over them. "Can you believe these? I see clearance in their future." She turned the pricing sheet over and saw that they were selling for eight dollars for the set. "Or maybe not. They're only eight bucks."

Stephanie, one of Lavender's closest friends, came into the store with a cupcake for Lavender.

"Snack!" Stephanie exploded with electricity, handing the treat to Lavender.

"Thanks, Steph. You'd better scoot, Mr. Magoo is coming in any minute from his lunch." Mr. Magoo was Lavender's nickname for the store owner, Mr. Baldwin.

Steph took her advice and said they'd talk later. She waved goodbye to Jenny on her way out the door.

A young woman came in, browsing the lingerie racks. Lavender noted the items that she took away from the rack as she continued to browse the store for perfume and body hugging workout pants. 20 minutes later the woman was ready to check out.

"I'll grab this one, Jenny," Lavender said

helpfully.

Jenny glanced up absently from where she was pricing the new pajamas on the round rack. "Sure."

Lavender made pleasant conversation with the customer, talking about the new workout shoes they were getting in next week that were really great quality for the price they were selling them for. The woman smiled and said she'd probably come back to see them.

Behind the register Lavender keyed in Jenny's code. She slipped the panties she'd had her eye on into her pocket after she desensitized them. She finished the check out cheerfully. The woman left smiling.

Lavender was careful to space out what she took, and careful to make sure it looked like Jenny was on the register when it happened.

Jenny finished out her shift, glad to go home and wait for her call from Jim. His class had returned from France this morning. They had exchanged e-mails and a couple of phone calls but it still felt like it had been forever since they really talked.

Chapter 29

Carter pulled his truck to the curb of the Carapelli house for their first Wednesday night tasting in a couple of weeks. He'd come to really look forward to those nights.

"Thanks for letting me drive, dad."

"What's the point in having a license and a truck if you don't get to drive? It's nice to share the chores with you, too." It had been one of those growing up moments for him, realizing that his son needed a chance to gain from his own experiences instead of just hearing lectures from him about what he had seen and done.

"Is tonight only about dessert, dad? That doesn't seem like Dana. I thought she'd tell us to eat dinner first."

"There's dinner, too. The book takes that into consideration. The idea is that the dinner cooks with the desserts so the cook can do both at the same time. I'm thinking casserole type stuff. Whatever it is, I'm trusting it will be great." Joe went to ring the doorbell.

Jenny opened the door with a big, happy smile. It didn't fall even if it was Jim she wanted to see most. She wanted to see them, too. "Hi."

"It smells amazing in here," Joe sniffed at the cinnamon laced air.

"We're doing the morning baking part of the book tonight. We'll be eating baked French toast, baked apple pancakes, pumpkin cinnamon muffins, stuff like that. I haven't had a bite of anything yet. I just got home."

Jason heard them and added in that his anticipated mini pecan tarts were part of the menu tonight.

The stunning array of dishes were already on the dining room table. The teens flocked to it, talking about what they would like the most.

"Dana," Joe turned the corner and held himself in place, watching her juggle what looked like twenty pans.

"Are you early? Or am I late?" Dana asked, pushing hair out of her eyes with her elbow.

"We're early. I was going to take a look at that dog house idea Jason was asking me about. We have one at the ranch and the dogs really liked it when it was cool at night. They liked to sit on top of it." He shook his head. "I've never seen dogs do that, Dana, but it gave me an idea for a project for Jason, Carter, and I. I'm guessing they didn't mention we'd be here early tonight?"

She put her hands behind her back so she wouldn't get the sticky stuff on her hands all over him. "Thank you, again. Yes, they do want a dog house. Jenny mentioned it to me. I didn't know you'd be here early but this seems to be my year for great surprises." She sauntered forward to kiss him hello.

"Mmmm. You taste like cinnamon. It's fun to see you in action. It's usually all cleaned up when I get here." He enjoyed the kiss that left her vulnerable with her hands behind her back. They were finding a kiss that let them touch each other a little in front of the kids without things getting too steamy. It was much more satisfying than a chaste kiss and a hug.

The doorbell sounded.

"You'll get to meet Brittany now. You're about to see how it gets cleaned up so well. She's worth her weight in gold."

Carter was closest to the door. Dana tagged him to let Brittany in. "Could you get that for me, Carter?"

Carter opened the door for Brittany, letting go of the odd feeling that he was treating the Carapelli's house like his own.

He swallowed loudly when he saw Brittany. She was dressed in shorts, sandals, and a tank top. She wore something subtle that reminded him of a tester Jenny had put under his nose at Hot Topic on City Walk.

"Now I have to wash up. I'm not that far behind, thank goodness. I have something for Brittany from the trip. All I need to do is put the filling in those cupcakes."

"Put the filling in the cupcakes?" Carter asked as he and Brittany joined Joe and Dana in the kitchen.

"Yeah. You know when you mail or travel with frosted things they tend to get messy. This way there's no chance of that. It also means less sugar in the batter because you get a hit of sugar when your tongue hits the creamy center."

"That's another great idea, Dana." Brittany glanced over the dishes in the sink. "This doesn't look too bad. You're not trying to take it easy on me, are you, Dana?" She teased.

"If only I could've, Brittany. There was just too much to do. You know, maiden voyage and all. I spent most of the day recording and adjusting."

"By the way, I'm Joe, Dana's fiancé, this is my son, Carter." He helped the kid out, seeing how his tongue froze when he looked at Brittany. He hoped for his son's sake that she was as sweet as Dana or she'd be wreaking havoc on his son every time he saw her. When a woman looked like that she could learn to treat people well, or she could learn to use them. His money was on Dana not having a femme fatale in her house.

Brittany gaped at the announcement. "You're engaged? When did that happen? The last guy I remember you dating was Principal Howe."

"Principal Howe?" Carter asked, surprised.

Dana nodded, distracted by the various bowls of filling in front of her. "Yes to both." She concentrated on the choices and decided to take advantage of the fact that she had so many people to try her ideas out on.

Her voice activated recorder blinked on as she spoke. "Okay, opinions, please. I have strawberry, chocolate, vanilla, lemon, and coffee flavored filling. They can go into strawberry, chocolate, or vanilla flavored cupcakes. What combination sounds best to you?"

Joe took a spoon and dipped it in the coffee filling. "God, Dana, that's incredible. I'd want this in the vanilla cupcake. Have I mentioned I think you're amazing?"

"Awe," Brittany watched them, misty eyed. "Dana, you're in love. Congratulations." She turned to Joe and Carter. "It's great to meet you both. I'm Brittany."

"Isn't it great?" Dana beamed her happiness.

Carter hid his happiness for his dad and Dana by voting passionately for a chocolate filled strawberry cupcake.

Brittany shared her enthusiasm for chocolate by voting for chocolate in chocolate.

Jenny heard the group in the kitchen and joined in with a second for chocolate in chocolate.

The doorbell rang again. "Are you expecting anyone else, Dana?" Joe tasted each of the fillings, completely enjoying the way his workdays ended now that he felt like they could spend more time together. He'd been hesitant to push for more time together before the engagement.

"It's Jim!" Jenny squealed on her way to let him in.

"They haven't seen each other since he left for France," Dana reminded them.

"Can I help with this?" Carter asked, watching Dana push filling through tubes into the cupcakes. He couldn't see a hole when she finished.

Dana was pleased that he would want to. "Of course. There's enough here for all the combinations, I think. I want to skip the strawberry lemon and the strawberry coffee." She shuddered. "Unless anyone has a strong urge to try them."

Joe shared her shudder. "No thanks. You know, this is something else we have in common, love. We both love what we do. We're not watching the clock

The Dreaming

waiting to be doing something else just so we get a check. We enjoy every minute." He found new things to love about her all the time.

Dana nodded, agreeing. She gave Carter a tube of his own and showed him how to fill it and how to squeeze the filling into the tiny hole she made in the cupcake with the decorating tip.

"Hi," Jim walked into the kitchen, holding hands with Jenny.

"Hi," or "Hey," or "Hello," came back to him from different mouths.

"It's good that you have such a big kitchen, Dana." Brittany was at the sink rinsing what she could.

"I did have to have a big kitchen. I've always spent a lot of time in the kitchen."

"Can you cook like your mom?" Jim asked Jenny, watching the table and the kitchen wide eyed.

"Very few people can cook like my mom. That's why she sells so many books. I think I do okay. She made sure that we never have to depend on packaged foods." Jenny put the same undesirable emphasis on packaged foods that Dana did when she talked about them.

"So you cook, too, Jason?" Carter asked, carefully guiding vanilla into the various cupcakes.

"Yeah." He seemed unimpressed with the idea. "Before we had jobs we had to do this thing where

Jenny and I each had to cook dinner one night a week. She helped us learn."

Dana watched Carter with a teacher's eye and applauded his efforts. "You're a natural, Carter. Pastry takes a lot of patience. If you like you can take over the vanilla filling for me."

She looked over the group she had assembled in the kitchen, counting seven heads. "We'll make seven of each combination. With all of us I'm sure nothing will go to waste. I want to see what it's like to eat them, you know? Are they messy, do they fall apart. People will want to take these to parties so they should be neat when you eat them."

"I thought you were going to talk about building a doghouse for Peaches and Cream?" Jenny asked, eyes roving over the table.

"We will." Joe answered.

"Why don't you go ahead? I'll stay here and help Dana." Carter's mind was clearly on his task.

"I'd like to help with the doghouse. What about you, Jim?" Jenny asked, happy to have him there. It was his first Wednesday at the house.

"Building's cool with me," he answered, following Jenny out of the kitchen.

"Let's go look at the backyard, then. When should we be back to eat, love?" Joe kissed her ear as he asked.

"Fifteen minutes should do it. I want everything

The Dreaming

to be warm."

Chapter 30

"Did you get what you needed from us, love?" Joe leaned back against the chair at the dining room table. "I'm hoping so because I can't eat another bite."

"But you feel okay, right?" She moved an experienced eye over him, looking for nausea or sweating.

He laughed. "No, love, I don't have indigestion. I'm just stuffed."

"It's all great," Jim announced. "I wish I didn't have to leave but I have this thing with my mom and grandparents tonight. I have to get going." His apology was mainly for Jenny, but he included everyone in it.

"That's cool. It's a TV night anyway. The more people we have the more complicated it gets." Jason excused himself from the table, taking dishes to the dishwasher.

"What's TV night?" Carter asked.

The Dreaming

Brittany turned to listen to Dana's answer, too. She was usually too busy to stay after she cleaned, but she'd lucked out and stayed to eat tonight instead of taking her food with her.

"On Wednesday nights if none of us have plans we watch TV or movies together. We all have different taste so we take turns picking out what we watch. I almost always choose one of the Iron Chefs or a comedy." Dana joined Jason in clearing the table. "You three are welcome to stay."

"I'll be right back. I'm going to walk Jim out." Jenny told the group.

"It's time for me to go, too. I have an early class." She turned to Dana. "You were right about these summer classes being a bear. I'm only taking the ones I think I don't need a lot of instruction on."

She took the cash Dana handed her, and the souvenir from their trip. It was a book called "Food & Mood: The Complete Guide to Eating Well and Feeling Your Best" that Dana had been telling her about. The whole starving student thing had her waiting to buy it until she had "extra" money. Whatever that was. "Oh, Dana, thank you!"

"It's my pleasure." She walked Brittany to the door where Brittany turned and said goodbye to everyone.

"Give us a minute, would you, Dana?" Joe motioned Carter to the backyard to talk when

Brittany had gone.

"Do you want to stay? I know a lot is changing. I don't want you to feel...I don't know, resentful, I guess, or obligated. If you don't want to stay, we could go." A hot summer wind ruffled Joe's hair.

"I want to stay, dad. It sounds like fun. I don't even know what Iron Chef is." Carter assured his dad. "I like the way things are going."

Joe sighed, relieved. "I'm glad, Carter, because I want to stay, too. Let's go get some good spots on the couch." He paused, confused. "Where is the TV? I haven't seen one."

"Yeah, it's in the family room. They have everything in there. You're gonna love it." Carter walked into the house ahead of his dad.

"We'll stay, love. We appreciate the invitation, too. So, what are we watching?" He noticed that everything was already put away.

"Do we put their names in the box, mom?" Jason asked.

She nodded. "That makes sense to me. What we do is draw names. Whatever order they come out in is the order we watch in, until everyone's ready for bed."

"Mom fell asleep during Resident Evil." Jason's tone said that he thought that was impossible.

"I did," she admitted humbly when Joe and Carter looked disbelieving.

The Dreaming

* * *

Joe and Dana wrapped around each other comfortably through the evening. Carter took over the recliner with a manly appreciation for its padding. Jenny took the opposite end of the green sectional she shared with Joe and Dana. Jason curled on the love seat by himself.

Carter had drawn first and taken them into the entertaining world of Pirates of the Caribbean: The Curse of the Black Pearl.

Jenny picked Invader Zim next, treating Joe to Dana's raucous laughter and imitation of Gir nagging Zim. "Are you gonna make biscuits? Are you gonna make biscuits? Are you gonna make biscuits? Are you gonna make biscuits?" She had them all cracking up.

For Joe's choice he looked through their DVD rack and chose Men in Black. When Will Smith rapped the Carapelli's moved with it, snapping their fingers and clapping with the beat.

Halfway through MIB Dana noticed Carter falling asleep, and trying to stay awake.

"Joe," she murmured in his ear, "Carter's falling asleep. Should we invite him to spend the night? We have plenty of room."

"Can I stay, too, love?"

"You can," she purred, excited.

"This just keeps getting better and better," Joe

kissed the top of her head, then burst out laughing when Will Smith stepped on a cockroach to stop the bug from escaping in the spaceship.

Jason got up and stretched at the end of the movie, volunteering to put it away and turn everything off.

"Carter?" Dana asked the sleepy teen, "Where do you want to sleep? You can stay here, or go into Jason's room, or take the guest room. Your choice."

"We're staying, dad?" Carter yawned, lost the battle with his eyelids, and closed them again. "I'll stay here."

Dana laughed softly and brought a blanket and pillow from the closet to tuck him in.

"Night, Jenny. Night, Jase." Dana kissed them, then walked the house, checking for lights left on, open windows, or unlocked doors.

"Goodnight," Joe nodded to them, noticing that they were looking pretty tired.

"Night, mom. Night, Joe." Jenny disappeared into her room.

Jason sent a sort of wave at them and stretched out on the couch where he was with the TV remote in his hand.

"All set?" Joe asked, watching from the hallway.

"Umm hmm. Are you sleepy? Would you like me to tuck you into the guest room?" she teased.

"Snowballs chance," he flirted back.

The Dreaming

"If you insist, I can make some room for you."

"Your bed works just fine for me. Not that I've ever actually slept in it." He closed her door behind them, turned the lock.

"I have a new toothbrush in here." She offered it to Joe.

"That's handy." Joe took it from her and started to brush his teeth along with her in the side by side sinks. "I never knew why people got these but I'm liking this."

"The house came this way. I've never minded." Dana cleansed her face and added a moisturizer that smelled like aloe.

"Do you have a side?" Joe asked when they walked back to the bed.

"Honestly? The whole bed. I usually sleep alone."

Joe laughed. "Me, too. I guess we'll just see where we end up. You know, we've never spent the whole night together."

"I know. This is nice." Dana stood uncertainly by the bed, wondering whether she should change into lingerie.

"Come here, Dana, love." Joe laid on the bed, beckoning her.

She crawled across the bed to him, giggling when he pounced on her and pinned her underneath him.

Joe kissed her slowly, deeply, savoring the taste and feel of her. And the luxury of having the night to love her.

Dana felt her blood heat in response to him. To pound and throb. She ran her hands over his back, massaging. He groaned.

He reached for the button on her shorts, the zipper. He eased the white denim down her legs, following it with his lips. He paused at her feet, kissing her toes, rubbing his hands from thigh to arch.

He traveled up to her belly, lingering over her belly button, kissing. His hands swept beneath her and found her firm round cheeks. "Your body is such a miracle, Dana. If I didn't already love your food I'd have to make a better effort. It does amazing things for you."

"Thanks," she breathed, hoping he would choose to love her breasts soon.

"Ummm, delicious," he murmured when he kissed the curve of her waist.

"It is," she agreed, enjoying the way he moved his lips and tongue over her. Her eyes popped open. "Uh, Joe, I don't have any condoms here."

"I can go get some," he assured her.

"Or not-"

"I don't want to waste this night." He interrupted.

"I don't either. It's just that, well, I'm not fertile right now, so we don't really need a condom."

He raised himself onto his arms, thinking over what she was saying. "Are you sure we're not risking a pregnancy? That's the only reason I can think of that we need a condom."

Dana nodded her head. "I'm sure. I've been using the method forever. I only got pregnant when I wanted to. When we started making love I started tracking things again."

Joe was certain that Dana would never say it if it wasn't true. "Well then," he lifted her tank top, pushing his hands under the cups of her bra. He found her nipples and played with the hard tips, sending shocks through her.

"No fair," Dana argued. "You still have your shorts on."

Joe rolled to his back and pointed at his lower half. "It's all yours."

"It certainly is, and I promise to take very good care of it." Her hands moved to his zipper. She pulled it down, eyes on his. She released him, fully erect, from his shorts and boxers. She moved over his face, her lips taking his in a wet, passionate kiss while her hand stroked him expertly.

"You are amazing," he moaned. "A little too good. I want to be inside you right now." He lowered to her thighs and slid her panties down and off her legs. His tongue lathed between her thighs, tasting that she was just as ready as he was.

"Come here, Joe," she urged him up to meet her lips in a hot kiss. Her legs wrapped around his hips, angling up to invite him inside.

He pushed into her, moving in long, deep strokes. She threw her head back, moaning throaty words of appreciation for how he made her feel.

Joe stroked deeper, harder, when Dana gripped him deep inside of her. His moans grew louder. The headboard knocked against the wall, loud and rhythmic.

Dana froze.

"What, love? Is something wrong?" He forced himself to hold still.

"We, uh, we need to pull the bed away from the wall, Joe. We'll wake everyone if the walls are knocking. And you're going to have to be quieter. You're loud." Her words were apologetic and embarrassed.

Joe had to laugh at her expression. "You're right, love. We've never made love with anyone else around. I'm surprised they didn't pound on the walls at the hotel."

"You know, I was, too." Remembering their lusty night brought her back to getting back to it. She got up and motioned for Joe to get off the bed so they could move it from the wall.

The Dreaming

"You do something to me that I've never experienced. I've never been too noisy or rocked a headboard that hard against the wall. If that's normal for you, I don't want to know about it." Joe growled, pulling her back under him.

"Kiss me," she urged, soothing him with her mouth. "Touch me, Joe." She pushed him to his back. "You're by far the best lover I've ever known." She eased over him, lowered onto him. She moved her hips up and down, pulling her top and bra off. She reached behind her to stroke him, feeling the wet heat she left on his cock.

He stroked his fingertips over her nipples, sitting up to take the hard peak in his mouth. He sucked hard, guiding her hips to stroke faster up and down his cock.

"God, Dana," he moaned against her flesh in ecstasy. He kept his mouth closed to muffle his increasingly loud moans of pure pleasure.

"Oh, yeah," she moaned to him softly, bouncing fast as she convulsed against him.

He flipped her onto her back, pounding into her, feeling her walls squeeze around him. He spurted his release into her, moaning, panting.

"Now if only we could get each other off in bed, we'd have it all." He teased.

"Why do you do that?" She inquired in a sleepy voice.

"Because you're the best lover I've ever had."

"You tell jokes after sex because I'm the best lover you've ever had?" Her lips curved up in a confused smile.

He laughed. "I thought you were asking why I respond to you the way I do."

"Okay, so then why?" She cuddled up to him, slipping under his arm. She licked beads of sweat from his neck.

"You know, that's something you bring out in me, too. I guess it's just that I have such a great time."

"Am I really the best?" She felt her body start to tingle again. She wanted to bring him there with sexy, flirtatious kisses and words.

"Hands down, by a mile, there's no one that ever came close to you." He answered in a calm, relaxed voice.

She kissed him again, lingering over the way his lips curved up in a satisfied smile. "Take a nap, Joe. I'm not done with you."

Chapter 31

"How did you and Lucy meet?" Joe asked from the driver's seat as they followed the directions on the navigator Dana gave him as an engagement present.

"We met in a biology class. She was my assigned lab partner." She watched the green trees that lined the freeway pass by her window. Garth Brooks sang on the radio.

"When?"

"Our first year of college. We had the same major so we hit it off right away." She turned away from the window to watch him.

"I didn't know you went to college. What was the major?"

"Nutrition. Are you surprised?"

"Somehow, no." He grinned. "So now you write cookbooks and she reviews restaurants for a syndicated column?"

"It's the closest we could stay to food, I guess. Lucy got me my first job as a nutritionist. She got her position at the hospital and recommended me the minute a new position opened up. We worked together until I left on maternity. Lucy left the hospital because she couldn't agree with what she was being asked to do."

"Like what?"

"Like the sodium counts in the food, and not providing strict enough counseling for patients. They needed to learn how to eat right and her hands were pretty tied as to what she could say."

"Interesting. I know that when my dad had his stroke a nutritionist visited his room, talked to him and mom about exercise."

"That's a holistic approach," Dana commented.

"Like your approach to birth control, right? How did you start that? It's very much appreciated, by the way. Condoms aren't my favorite unless we need them. Then I'll wear them gladly. I'm not exactly in a position to complain." He smiled wolfishly.

"I didn't do well on the pill. I tried it when Ben and I started having sex but it made me sick. I looked at alternatives and got good at the natural planning method. A woman's body is really clear about when it's fertile and when it isn't. Nearly everything changes."

"I trust you to know your own body. I like getting to know it, too." He leered at her.

"If you start that we're going to have to find a

quiet place to talk about it." She flirted back.

"Good point. You turn on fast. It doesn't take much."

"I guess you're just that hot." She changed the subject before she started thinking of where they could slip off to be alone enough for what was forming in her mind. "Joe, have you ever found out why I have limited questions in The Dreaming?"

"Chicken," he teased.

"Better a chicken than arrested for having sex in public."

"Hmm, I see your point." He looked over at her sitting there in her pretty blue sun dress and low strappy heels. His mouth watered.

"Joe?" She laughed.

"The Dreaming, right. I've never been able to find anything on that. I think if you want to know you're going to have to ask You." The robotic tone on the dashboard sounded and said "Exit, right, at Riverside Drive, ½ mile."

"I love this thing, Dana. Your dad told me you have a thing for electronics. I didn't see what he meant until I saw your family room. You have a sweet set-up in there."

"I'm glad you like it since we'll be combining households in a few months."

He caught her worried tone. "It'll be fine, love. Everyone's already adjusting. No one thought it was weird for Carter and I to be there this morning."

"Thank goodness."

"Oh, my, god, Dana. He's incredible!" Lucy held her verdict until Joe excused himself to the restroom.

"Isn't he though?"

Dana's dreamy smile pleased Lucy. "You deserve it, D. You deserve to be happy and cherished."

Dana held Lucy's hand across the table, highlighting the ring on her finger.

"Is that what I think it is?" Lucy asked. "Already?"

Dana was used to it now, so she nodded calmly and repeated her new sound bite. "We're old enough to know we shouldn't waste time on formalities." She added the next part for Lucy, who had known her since she met Ben. "Besides, look how long I dated Ben before we got married. That's no insurance policy."

"Hmm. You're sure?" Lucy knew Dana made good decisions. She had learned to develop good instincts about people.

"I've got the ring. We also have a date and I'd like to know if you'll be my maid of honor."

"Oh, god, D. Of course I will. Wow. I'm sorry if I sounded like a mom there. It was hard watching you with Ben after awhile. You seemed so lonely."

The Dreaming

"I was lonely. And bored. At least I got the twins from it, right?"

"Right. Here he comes."

He slid uneasy glances at the industrial juicers The Shake Shack sported on its counters. Juicers filled with green goo from what he could see.

"I'm glad to meet you, Lucy. I hope I can say the same about the restaurant."

"They have a menu, not just liquids. Still, I thought we should try a large shot of wheat grass to get things started. You in?"

"Will I like that?" He asked Dana.

"Possibly. You can give me yours if you don't."

"Okay then."

The waitress walked over to them casually. "Do you know what you want yet?"

"We'll take three large wheat grass shots, and one of each of your specials. What's the best thing on your menu?" Lucy handled the ordering.

"The seitan skewers with Thai peanut sauce. It's an appetizer." She answered immediately, sure of herself.

"We'll take an order of that, and the Thai salad to go with it. We'll be sharing those. What do you guys want to drink?"

Dana glanced at the tea menu in front of her. "A chai latte, cold, with soy."

"Iced tea, regular," Joe put in.

"Waters for all of us and I'll try the organic iced coffee, soy, please."

"One check?" The name badge identified her as Laura.

"Please. My treat." Lucy smiled to Dana and her new betrothed.

Dana snorted when Laura was out of earshot. "Your treat my ass." She turned to Joe. "It's all paid for. Part of the job."

"You couldn't let me look generous for one afternoon, D?" Lucy pouted playfully.

"I already told him about how you got me my first nutrition job," she soothed.

The wheat grass arrived and Joe shook his head at the women. "I'm not even sure my horses would drink this."

They laughed and drank their green shots.

"Very good," Dana voted.

"Perfect temperature," Lucy agreed.

"That's right, this is my second day in a row of looking at food from all the angles, right? You never get tired of it, do you, Dana?"

She shook her head, happy.

He tested his green juice with a small sip, then swigged it back. He felt satisfied by it in some way. "It feels good."

"Exactly!" Lucy beamed. "Can I quote you?"

"Sure. So tell me, what's the deal with the

appetizer. I heard her say that we'd be eating Satan." He shook his ear like he was checking his hearing.

"It's more like say-tan. It's made out of wheat," Dana laughed with him.

When the drinks and appetizers arrived they passed them around, letting Joe try things for the first time. It was fun for Lucy and Dana to see his expressions when he tasted new things. They'd been into it for so long they forgot what it was like when they first started.

"I enjoyed that," Joe told her as he dropped her off at home with a deep kiss.

"We got lucky. Sometimes those places try really hard and fall very flat. They're doing it well."

"Lucky for me. Do you and Lucy run into a lot of bad food in her work?"

"Not really. Mediocre is usually the worst we get."

"That's good. I'm going to get back to work. You know where to find me, and I encourage you to do that often. I like having you around." He took another kiss, pleased at the little shiver she responded with.

Chapter 32

"You wished to see me?" You asked, monotone.

"What's that?" Dana looked around her, seeing that she was in her own bedroom. She could see that her alarm clock glowed green and read 12:12.

"Are you asking me?" You answered.

Right. You. The Dreaming. "No. I need a moment." She checked herself and saw that she was wearing a nightgown. That helped. She stretched and yawned in her sleep, shaking more awareness into herself.

"Now, what did you say?"

"I was told by Joe that you wish to see me? That you have a question."

"You know, I do have a question. I want to know why my questions are limited, and yes I do think it's funny to use a limited question to ask that question."

You floated, unblinking. "You are limited in your questions because you need to experience and figure things out on your own."

"Okay," she nodded. "I can accept that. I don't have any more questions. And thank you."

"Do you wish to return to your sleep now? Or will you be exploring?"

"I'll be...going to Joe." She considered, then asked, deeming her questions worthy. "But first I'd like to know if I can see if Sue is a threat to my son."

You shook his head no. "She is not."

Dana relaxed. "I appreciate that."

"You're welcome."

"Last question of the night. I'd like to go to Joe. How do I do that?"

"Think of where you want to be to go there. Focus."

"Thanks again. We'd like to be...alone."

"I understand. I will leave the two of you alone tonight."

"Thanks again."

Trying her new skill, Dana thought of Joe's bedroom, of him lying in his bed. She focused, closing her eyes and really hoping.

"Dana?" Joe looked up at her, floating above his bed. "What are you doing?"

"I...oh, wow." She laughed. She imagined herself on the bed with Joe and was there instead. "I'm learning to come visit you. You is taking the night off."

"So we're alone?" He scanned the room.

"We are. What did you want to do to me in the truck today, Joe?"

He grinned his wolfish smile and pushed her nightgown up.

The first of July rolled in lazily for Dana. She woke feeling satisfied from her dream loving with Joe. It was better than she'd guessed it would be, and her guesses had been pretty amazing.

The knock sounded on her door again, reminding her of why she had woken up in the first place.

"I'm leaving for work, mom. You slept late." Jenny did a turn in front of her. "Do you like it?"

Dana approved the white knee length skirt and scarlet tank top. "The sandals are...mine, right?" She narrowed her eyes.

"Oops. I meant to ask."

She relaxed. "I know you'll take good care of them. What time will you be home?"

"About 3:30."

"Sounds good. How are things with Lavender?"

"Normal. I think you're wrong about her, mom. Maybe your dream meant something else."

She rested on the pillows another moment, considering. "Just hang in there for me a little longer. I don't know why just yet."

"If you say so. See ya!"

The Dreaming

* * *

It was payday and Lavender had the day off. Jenny worked alongside Claire, Mr. Baldwin's daughter.

Claire stepped out for lunch, telling Jenny that she'd be back in an hour.

Jenny tried to fill the time, but there just wasn't that much to do. She pulled out her phone and texted to Cat about going to the lake with her family on the fourth.

Lavender came in twenty minutes into Claire's lunch. "Hey, you. Nice sandals."

"Thanks. They're my mom's." Her phone signaled that Cat was responding.

"I'll let you get that. I'm going to grab my check out of the office."

"Sure," Jenny answered, distracted. Cat's parents said she could go with Jenny's family. "Awesome!" she texted back.

One of their regular customers came in, asking if they had her hold items. She had run out of time the other day and asked for the items she'd tried on to be put aside until she could come back and buy them. The transaction took about twenty minutes by Jenny's estimation. She was glad that it ate up some of the time. They were s-l-o-w today.

Lavender came out of the office and waved to Jenny from the door. "I'll see you tomorrow, Jenny. Gotta run."

Jenny frowned, thinking of what Lavender could have been doing in the office for all that time. Maybe she made a call or something. She shrugged and looked for something to do.

Mr. Baldwin came into the store then and asked Jenny if she'd taken her lunch yet.

"No. Should I go now? I'm hungry."

"That's fine. When did Claire leave?"

"I don't remember exactly but I think she should be back very soon."

Mr. Baldwin smiled and told her to go ahead, and to enjoy her break.

Jenny went across to the juice place and ordered a smoothie with all fresh fruit. She drank it quickly. Her breaks weren't that long.

Mr. Baldwin met her at the door when she walked in. "Jenny, did anyone go into the office while I was gone?"

"Yeah, Lavender came in for her check."

"That makes sense. Did she say anything to you? Or do anything unusual?"

Jenny thought back to how much time she had spent in the office. "Yeah, she was in there for a long time."

"She didn't say anything about why or what she was doing?"

"Nothing, Mr. Baldwin. Is something wrong?"

"Yes, there is. There's money missing.

The Dreaming

Yesterdays cash deposit. I'm waiting for Claire to come back with the code to check the camera."

"Camera? I didn't know you had one in there. Oh, well, I think it's good you have that."

Mr. Baldwin watched her carefully, all of his senses told him that she wasn't the one taking things. Still, she was on register when they had complaints. "We put it in because we suspected that we had a problem. We didn't tell anyone for the same reason."

"Hey, dad. I'm ready," Claire walked into the store and said a calm hello to Jenny. The two went into the office.

Half an hour later they walked out and told her that they would like her to stay late for the interview with the police. The tape clearly showed Lavender searching for, and taking, the missing money.

"Sure, I'll stay. I just need to call my mom to let her know why I'll be late." She was shaking as she made the call.

Dana hung the receiver in the cradle, stunned by Jenny's news.

Chapter 33

Dana opened the priority mail package that her mailman brought to the door. It was from her parents. She unwrapped the box inside the box and found that her mother had made an album of their visit, from start to finish. The pictures moved her, as she knew they would the rest of the family. The last picture in the album, of her on Moonlight wearing her new black hat, jiggled her memory of seeing the exact same picture of herself in the book You showed her and Joe in The Dreaming.

Dana tried to remember what the other pictures had been of. Since the truth about Lavender had come out, and the way Sue faded from their lives without a trace, she was paying a lot more attention to what she had seen in The Dreaming.

She continued to unpack the box, finding a separate album for Jenny, Jason, and Carter. The card said that someday they would be on their own so they should have their own memories to take with

The Dreaming

them. They were wrapped so Dana would wait for them to open them.

She looked at the picture of her sitting on Moonlight again and it reminded her, oddly, of Ivy from New York. It was Ivy that had been wearing the lavender oil that had clicked Riddle's clue into place for her. She dug out the number for Ivy and dialed, unsure of what to say exactly. She also remembered thinking that she saw Ivy as a shadowy figure in The Dreaming.

"Hello?" A male voice greeted her.

"I'd like to speak to Ivy, please. It's Dana Carapelli."

The man whistled, impressed. "Really? Ivy said you asked for our number. Hold on, she's right here."

Dana listened to the man run to get Ivy. She heard his words through the phone. "You'll never guess who's calling! No, I won't tell you. It's a good surprise."

"Hello?" Ivy asked, sounding sleepy.

"Hi, Ivy, it's Dana Carapelli. How are you?"

Ivy squealed in her excitement. "Awesome! I had a feeling I would hear from you!"

"Those kinds of feelings are what I'm calling you about. I'd like to talk to you about that."

"I'd love to talk about it with you. Just a sec."

Dana listened to the sounds of a nursing baby

come across the phone, the sweet little breathless slurps and sighs. She melted.

"You had your baby," she sighed happily.

"Yes, she's early, but if she'd stayed in longer she would have been too big. She's just right, aren't you, Rose?"

They listened to the sweet baby sounds together.

"I love being a mom," Dana shared.

"I got that from your books. You always include everyone in everything. That's another reason I like them. I grew up like that."

"Did you grow up intuitive?" She sipped from her water as they talked, suddenly reminded of how thirsty she got when she had nursed the twins.

"Slightly so. It came on more fully later when I started taking yoga and learning to meditate. How did you learn?"

"I didn't. I just woke up one day, after a vivid dream, and found out that I could telepath with my fiancé. He's been helping me with this."

"You're lucky. My husband likes all of it but doesn't have the same experiences I do."

"That's why I called, to ask you if you think we've shared a dream. I think we did, after we met."

"I thought so, too," Ivy sounded thoughtful. "The difference is that I wasn't dreaming. I was meditating. There's this place I go when I want to. It's really relaxing and there's a man there, with really white hair. He tells me things."

"I know him. His name is You. I've also heard him called Father Time."

"I didn't know he had a name. That's cool."

"Could you help me learn how to go there when I want to? I'd like to learn to navigate my dreams. My fiancé can. He was born with the ability."

"I'd love to. As these things go it makes sense that we'll be there this weekend for a spiritual parenting seminar. We wouldn't have been able to go if she was on time because they wouldn't let me fly that late in the pregnancy. They had just enough room for us. I really felt like we needed to go." She laughed sleepily.

"Here? In Joshua Tree?"

"Yes. We're leaving in a couple of hours to go to the airport."

"That is excellent timing. When could we meet?"

"Sunday is the last day of the retreat, and we only have one morning class. After that we weren't sure what we would do."

"Would you be comfortable coming to my house? I think it's good for what we're planning." Dana couldn't believe her luck, or the timing of everything.

"We'd love that. Could you e-mail the directions to my cell phone from the events center? Do you know it?"

"It's just down the highway from my house. Yes, I'll send them. What's the number? Thanks again, Ivy. I really appreciate your help in this."

"My pleasure. Besides, I'm already learning from you. I have been for years."

Dana was touched.

"Joe?"

"Yes, love?"

Dana went soft inside at how sweet he sounded, how fully warm and welcoming.

"I have a question about Sunday. Can you come over, alone?"

"Sure, love. I'm always up for alone time with you." *He laughed at his corny joke.*

"As great as that would be, I have another reason for asking. I met a fan in New York, at a signing, when you and I were telepathing. Remember when I said I had to go?"

"Yes, I do."

"Well, she and her family are coming here on Sunday so she can teach me more ways to control what happens in The Dreaming. She doesn't go there in her sleep, she meditates to get there. I'd like you to meet her."

"Interesting. Sure, I can do that. Should we plan on spending the night that night? We'll get an

earlier start if we leave from one place."

"Nice tactics, sexy. That's just your latest way of spending the night making love with me, but I'll take it."

Joe leaned back in his saddle on Medallion's back. They'd been out for a fast ride, one that they were finding was making them better partners.

"Do I need tactics to spend the night with you, love?" He teased.

"You seem to set it up with practical reasoning every time."

"That's because you're a practical woman. If you'd rather be seduced I can do that."

"You seduce me plenty, Joe. I'm not complaining." She sighed nervously, thinking about the coming trip.

"It's going to be great, Dana. They'll love you. How could they do anything but love you?"

"I appreciate that, Joe. Meeting your whole family like this, camping for two days, is overwhelming me when I think about it."

"I promise I'll be there the whole time. If anyone is out of line I'll be right there. I'm only a thought away."

"That does help. So we're set for Sunday?"

"We are. What time do you want me there?"

Dana had a great lunch ready for Ivy, Tracey, and

Joe. It was a fun chance to cook something fancy. She didn't get to do that very often.

The doorbell sounded. Dana went to get it, keeping the dogs in the back part of the house since she didn't know if the baby would be okay around them. She knew they loved babies and wouldn't want to leave her alone.

"Hey, love," Joe stepped in with a bouquet of long stemmed, red roses.

"Joe, you just, wow, you are so thoughtful." She thanked him with a deep, wet kiss.

"When will they be here? Any chance they called and said they'd be an hour late? I could do some 'thoughtful' things with you in an hour." He telepathed so he wouldn't have to break the kiss.

"No, sexy, it'll have to wait until we go to bed tonight. Sorry," she said, and she meant it.

"It just gives me something to look forward to. Besides that lunch. You amaze me, over and over again."

The doorbell sounded again. Dana opened it to greet the smiling family on her porch.

Their afternoon passed rapidly. Over lunch they spoke of various experiences they had with shared dreams.

Joe told them things they didn't know about The Dreaming, about how vast it was. He'd been exploring it his whole life and he was still finding new parts of it. Tracey was basically openly envious but didn't have too many experiences of his own to share. Ivy taught all of them ways to get into a deep, meditative state.

Joe loved seeing Dana hold the newborn baby. She was such a natural mother. Everyone she came into contact with was embraced and nurtured. Rose accepted her as easily as she did her own parents.

Ivy took her camera out and snapped pictures of Dana holding her fresh smelling little bundle. They spit out of her portable dock instantly.

Joe sat beside her with the drying picture. "Look at this, love. Remember?"

"It was the night you confirmed that I'm your soul mate." The picture was just as it had been in The Dreaming.

"What?" asked Ivy.

"Dana and I saw this picture in The Dreaming. It was, let's see, the night before the signing, I think. That fits with what happened with Dana and I. She and I met the day after she was in The Dreaming for the first time."

That had Dana shivering, because she was certain now that the third picture they had seen was of her standing next to Carter in a hospital bed.

Joe felt her, and rubbed her arm in comfort. "I know about that one, Dana. He's not going to be hurt or anything like that. He's going to be acting."

"How do you know?" Dana and Ivy asked at the same time. Tracey was impressed beyond anything he'd ever seen by the bond his wife shared with one of his personal heroes.

"I asked. When I saw the picture I looked into it. I found the answer right away. It's for drama club. Carter hasn't mentioned joining yet, but he will. Soon, I'd guess, from what we're seeing by these pictures. Remember when I asked you about pregnancy? This picture was the reason for my question. I didn't want to take a chance on getting you pregnant. We never discussed whether we wanted to look at the option. For all I knew, you wanted to have another baby."

"No, Joe, I don't. I'm very happy with the three we have now." She caressed his face tenderly, shared a gentle kiss. Rose fussed in her arms, making the "baby's pooping" face.

"I'm glad, Dana. That would have been tough for me, but if you really wanted it I would have made the effort to get used to the idea."

"I think it's Tracey's turn to change her," Ivy said, picking Rose up out of Dana's arms. "While they do that I want to give you a little gift. We'll have time to practice a little meditation, and then we'll have to go."

Ivy pulled a gift bag from her diaper bag, handing it to Dana.

The Dreaming

Dana found a bottle of homemade peach shampoo and a pot of homemade grape lip gloss inside. "Thank you. These smell wonderful!"

"That's what I like to make besides food. They're really good for your body, too."

Dana tried the lip gloss, sharing a kiss with Joe so he could test it with her.

"Very nice, Ivy. If you have other flavors I'll buy some. I'm always looking for gifts for my mom and sisters. Now I have Jenny to think of, too, and Meredith."

"That doesn't even start the list, Joe," Dana laughed. "Wait till we start looking at all the people we know when we blend our lives."

Ivy preened, truly flattered. "I've been wanting to start a professional distribution."

"I think you just did," Dana said, noticing a flash out of the corner of her eye.

Chapter 34

Dana ran through the techniques one by one as she prepared for a night in The Dreaming. She intended to go in alone and ask the question that she most wanted the answer to. Joe slept soundly, peacefully, beside her.

She wore a pretty blue nightgown that fell a few inches below her thighs. Her hair was clean and smelled like peaches thanks to Ivy's gift of homemade shampoo. She'd cleansed and moisturized her face. Her final touch was Ivy's nourishing grape lip gloss.

She eased her body away from any stress she might have built up during the day the way Ivy had taught her. She cleared her mind of any distractions or doubts, also courtesy of Ivy.

From Joe and You she had learned the importance of knowing where she wanted to go, and what she wanted to do there. She slipped a picture of the place in her mind. The one where she had seen

The Dreaming

pictures that accurately portrayed future events in her life.

She let herself drift into a sweetly scented, confident sleep.

And woke up in The Dreaming exactly where she had intended. You floated beside her.

"Good evening, You."

"Good evening, Dana."

She glanced around, noting only that instead of the book she had seen before, there were large, blank picture holders dominating the room. Everything else looked the same as any other visit.

Satisfied that everything was as she wanted it to be she turned to You.

"I have a question for you."

He floated, unblinking, expressionless.

Dana laughed to herself. Why she expected to see anything different from You she'd never know. He was unfailingly unchanging.

"I'd like to know how it is that I got so lucky. How did I end up with such a perfect life?"

You turned to one of the picture screens and a picture appeared on it of her and her dad when she was a little girl.

She and her dad walked along the path near the house they had lived in back then. She wore a pretty pink jumper and a pony tail that was just starting to hint at the chestnut color it was now.

George pointed to the night sky as he usually did on their evening walks. "There," his voice rose with excitement, "it's a shooting star, Dana. Hurry and make a wish. Don't tell anyone. That way it will come true."

Inspired by the fairy tale slumber birthday party for her friend Miriam the night before, Dana wished as hard as she could, with the full faith of an inspired, passionate child, to live happily ever after with her one true love.

Dana's eyes filled with tears as she watched the screen. She struggled to hold back the powerful emotions.

The movie zoomed in on the falling star then, and she saw You riding it on his hover board. The night sky around him inky black, the stars, his and the others, twinkling or glowing steady.

"Did you make your wish, sweet pea?" George inquired absently, thinking he should get her home. Tomorrow was a school day and she'd likely been up all night at the slumber party.

"I did, daddy. But like you said, I won't tell you what I wished for."

That night when she slept she dreamed of riding a white horse, tall in the saddle, with a black hat on her head.

Dana sniffled, recognizing Moonlight, her very first horse, the one she had a strong, instant bond

The Dreaming

with.

The screen went blank, then another lit to her right. She saw herself, and You, with a woman holding a clipboard.

"I will choose that one," You said. The camera angle changed, showing her what You was pointing at. A still picture of her standing there with her father, wishing on the star.

Dana tried to contain her emotions, and failed. She was sobbing openly, overwhelmed by what You had chosen to do for her.

She approached him for the first time ever and held out her arms in an invitation to hug him in gratitude.

You smiled. The entire room lit up like a stadium on a dark night. It was so bright Dana blinked against it.

"You're welcome," You monotoned.

Desert Sunrise
The Second Book in the Natural Gifts Series

Gina Briganti

Chapter 1

Lucy rose before the sun as she did each and every morning.

Today separated all others in previous memory, because today her best girlfriend, Dana Carapelli, was marrying the man she was made for, Joe Jacobs.

The adorable couple had planned a sunset wedding, on horseback.

In preparation for the ceremony Lucy had taken the lessons she needed to be up to the task as maid of honor.

The wedding clothes and food fit the couple perfectly. Jeans, boots, a sexy country blouse for Dana, and cowboy hats. The groom was wearing a tailored black western shirt with pearl buttons.

They would be eating barbecue, many of the dishes created for the occasion by the extremely talented bride.

Lucy made her way to Dana's kitchen, thinking

Desert Sunrise

how she'd never heard it this quiet. The Carapelli's didn't live here anymore. The last few days had been spent moving everyone to the ranch.

She and Dana had spent the night here, away from the banned eyes of the groom.

Dana had offered the house to other guests from out of town for tonight, but Lucy was the only one to take her up on it.

The teakettle sat glamorously on the professional stove. Dana would have left it out for her. She knew that with all of Lucy's natural energy starting the day with coffee would only make her edgy.

Lucy boiled the water, poured a cup of the special nourishing and soothing tea she made herself.

Teacup warm in her hand, Lucy stepped barefoot onto the back patio. She chose one of the padded lounges Dana kept there.

Dark turned to light, painting gorgeous strips of pink and orange across the lightening sky. In no time at all the sky would be an amazing blue, complete with fluffy white clouds.

She drained the tea slowly, knowing that she wouldn't be able to contain her energy any longer.

Thoughts began to race through her head like lightening. Her arms and legs started to thrum with energy. She was craving music and movement.

The day had begun.

Gina Briganti

* * *

"Lucy?" Dana went to the back patio, knowing that her friend would sit out there until she couldn't hold still anymore.

"Dana!" Lucy bubbled her greeting, making Dana giggle.

"That's the perfect greeting for my wedding day." Dana sat on a matching lounge nearby, glancing over the yard she wouldn't be looking at day after day anymore. She'd hardly been here for the last week between the move and the wedding.

The only reason she'd managed to wiggle loose from Joe last night was that the women of both families wouldn't hear of her spending the night in the house with the groom.

"Dana, I'm so happy for you!" The effervescence that Lucy carried everywhere with her colored her words.

"I'm so happy for me, too. I'm glad you're here to share it with me, Luce. It wouldn't be the same without you."

"I know I've had a heck of a schedule lately, but I wouldn't miss your wedding for the world. Somehow we managed to pull off the bridal shower. Tell me again why you didn't want a rehearsal?" Lucy's thoughts and questions came rapid fire, as always.

Desert Sunrise

"We didn't think there was enough to rehearse. Dinner at the 29 Palms Inn was enough for us. It gave most of us a chance to get to know one another. The only one to stay behind was Stan. He was taking care of a brand new colt, only two days old. Have you ever seen a newborn horse, Luce? They're about the cutest thing I've ever seen." Dana went misty eyed. It didn't matter if the baby was human or animal to her, they all choked her up.

"No, never." Who would have thought that her best girlfriend would end up living out her life as a rancher's wife? Lucy shook her head at her thoughts. It worked for Dana's answer, too.

Dana sighed, relaxing for what could be the only time possible today.

"What time do you want to go over there?"

"About 2:00, I think. There isn't that much to do. The less time I'm in the house the fewer chances Joe has to peek at me. He's not fond of this separation, especially since we spent every night of the last week there. He told me that he was glad this silly tradition only had us apart for one night." Dana shook her head at how hungry her fiancé was to be with her after a year of being together.

"He does seem extra amorous. Good for you, D. I know what you have together is much more suited to you than what you had with Ben."

"No kidding. Could you see Ben getting married on horseback at sunset and celebrating with a barbecue? Not only no way, but even I didn't know how much I would love the life that Joe and I are building together."

"You know what impresses me? Your connection to Carter. If I didn't know better I'd say you raised him, Dana. The two of you are as much like mother and child as you are with Jenny and Jason. You're all very lucky." Lucy didn't bother to disguise the wistfulness in her voice. It was no secret to either of them that Lucy was a romantic and wanted what Dana had in her own life.

"He is a child of my heart," Dana nodded in agreement, "even if he didn't come out of my body."

There was a point to Dana's words, Lucy knew. An old one. Dana had long felt that just because Lucy couldn't bear children naturally, that it shouldn't stop her in any way from adopting a child.

Essentially that was what Dana had done with Carter, and Joe with Jason and Jenny.

"I know, D, I know." Lucy sighed it.

"You okay? I didn't mean to bring you down."

They shared the laugh. Nothing, anywhere, could bring Lucy down. Show her a tragedy, and she'd show you all the people rushing to help the victims. Show her an abusive situation and she'd

Desert Sunrise

point out all the measures in place to prevent it that were still fairly new to our society, and how that meant that the abused one had a whole new chance to make it out of the situation that didn't exist even a few years ago. Show her a divorce, and she'd see a new beginning.

It was one of the reasons the two women bonded the way they did. Their spirits were insuppressible.

"So tell me, does Joe have any cute ranch hands or family coming to the wedding?"

Dana considered before answering. Joe did have a foreman whose looks and build could rival Joe himself if you weren't sloppy in love with Joe. But was he someone she would want to see Lucy with?

No. She shook her head for her own and Lucy's answer. Stan wasn't the forever type. Lucy was. She deserved what she had waited so long to experience.

Dana considered Stan for a few more moments before sharing her thoughts with Lucy. She knew that the minute Lucy laid eyes on him she would want to know why Dana hadn't mentioned him.

"It's like this, Luce. You're going to see an amazingly gorgeous specimen of manhood at the ranch. He's nice, too, like helps little old ladies cross the street, nice. And charming. I haven't seen a man, woman, child, or animal that didn't light up in his presence. And he lives in the bunkhouse so he's there all the time. He's Joe's foreman, Stan. Thing is, Lucy, Stan likes to look, sometimes touch, but he's never once talked about or come close to doing more than that with a woman. Plenty have tried, from what I hear. He's happy to be alone. I thought you should have the full story before he smiles at you and melts your brain." There was laughter in her eyes as she said it, but she meant it just the same.

"So there's no reason not to enjoy myself a little with him, is there, if there's an attraction? If he gets the Dana stamp of approval I know he's got to be good for something." Lucy's tone reminded Dana that she's a big girl now, and she could enjoy a man without thinking it was going somewhere. If she hadn't learned to think that way she would have grown bitter a long time ago.

"Dana, the right man is out there for me, and when the time comes I'll find him. Until then, well, I'm going to live. I know that you only had a few years on your own before you met Joe, but honey, I've had a lot more. I know what I'm doing."

Dana moved to Lucy's lounge and hugged her close, glad for this amazing woman that she could say anything to.

"So now that we're done with the sunrise part of the morning, what do you want to do next?" Lucy inquired.

"How about breakfast? I love that it's just you and I-"

"Uh, hi, mom." Jenny stepped onto the patio.

"Okay, I love that it's just us girls?" Dana asked her question that way.

"Mrs. Jacobs is here, too. So are Sandy, Dara, and grandma. They want to go to breakfast at the Inn. They had such a good time there last night, and it's a Jacobs' family tradition for the women of the family to have breakfast together on the wedding day."

"Where are they?" Dana made the adjustment from spending a morning Lucy and Dana style, to spending it with the women of her family and the women of the family she was joining today.

"In the living room." Jenny stood looking around at the house she had spent so many years in. She had only been a year old when they bought it. She didn't know any other home. She was fine with living at the ranch for her last year of high school.

Seeing her mom as happy as she was made up for anything that she might miss about the house they had lived in. The ranch was quickly becoming her home because her mother and brother were there. And her new brother and stepdad.

"There you are!" Marla Jacobs, the impressive

woman that had raised Joe into the wondrous man that he was, stood on the patio, hands at her hips.

"Marla, good morning." Dana greeted. "So we're going to breakfast, are we?"

"Yep. Time honored Jacobs' family tradition. Sam's mother dragged me out of bed the night after my party, pounding head and all, and took us all to eat. It turns out to be a pretty good tradition, doesn't it, girls?" She polled her daughters as they walked through the house that was partly furnished with what they hadn't brought to the ranch.

"I'd like to find out," Dara answered wistfully. She was the youngest marriageable Jacobs at 35, and the only one who hadn't married at all yet.

"No need to get married just to get a breakfast with the women in your family," Sandy told her sister quietly. "It's a lot less trouble just to ask them over."

Dara looked at her closely, surprised at the tone in her voice. She had thought that things were working well for Sandy and Micah, despite a couple of rocky points over the years.

Sandy ducked her head, whispering, "Not today, Dara. Today is for Joe and Dana."

"Dana, do you have what you need over there already? I don't know if we'll be getting back this way after breakfast. Why don't you go on and shower? We'll visit while you do. I see you still have juice and coffee here, and tea. Would you ladies like something to drink while Dana rinses her sleep away?" Meredith stepped in to get the day moving.

Meredith hosted with perfection. No one in the room wondered after that morning where Dana had learned to be such a gracious hostess.

* * *

The women arrived at Sunny Skies Stables as a group, Marla coordinating with Carter to be sure that Joe was tucked away somewhere while they brought Dana into the house to dress.

The ranch was breathtaking. Lucy hadn't expected any less. The sexy, dynamic rancher that Dana had paired up with wouldn't have settled for less than astonishing.

Lucy parked where Dana pointed, behind the main house. "You won't be leaving again until after the reception is over so there's no need to worry about anyone blocking you in. We're leaving the area in front of the house clear for the delivery trucks."

"Okay, D. Let's get you into Jenny's room." Lucy followed the women to where they would be guarding the door against the very anxious groom. It was cute how they couldn't be apart for two minutes.

Dana slipped into the bathroom to answer Joe. He'd been trying to talk to her all morning but she'd been surrounded by people the whole time and the long silences were too awkward to explain.

"Love? Where are they hiding you?"

"Now why would you say hiding?" She teased.

"Because I've been looking for you since last night. You feel like you're close. I didn't sleep well." He tried to sound pitiful.

"I did. You couldn't wake me up for sex even once last night." She tried to make it sound like she was relieved at having a night away from him. Truthfully, she'd missed being with him.

"Is that why you found me in The Dreaming and put on that show for me? I appreciated that, you know. You can do that anytime." But even in sleep she had been chaste the night before their wedding, stripping for him through a veil she made so that he could see her but not touch her. *"Of course, next time I expect to be able to thank you properly for the show."*

"It was my way of giving you the stripper you said you didn't want."

"I'll always want a stripper, if the stripper is you."

"See, I give you what you want, even in your sleep. Now go on, Joe Jacobs, we have secret female

things to do to get me ready for tonight."

"Tonight won't be about sleeping, love."

"You mean once we get into the room at the Inn it won't. Now go on."

"Never underestimate a sexually frustrated groom."

Dana smiled to him and then told him to scat. There were people everywhere and things to do.

FROM THE AUTHOR

I have loved reading and writing all of my life. It has been a tremendous pleasure to write this story and share it with all of you.

I live in beautiful Southern California with my family, a special soul who masquerades as a dog, and the beautiful desert.

I welcome you to join me on goodreads and facebook.

Proof

Made in the USA
Charleston, SC
08 June 2013